Daria's Duke

By Linda Shenton Matchett

Chapter One

"Stealing is a new low for you, Pansy." Daria Burke thrust her clenched fists into the pockets of her skirt. Her hands tore through the worn fabric, exacerbating her foul mood. "That dress doesn't belong to you, so give it back."

Petite and exotic-looking, with ebony hair and green eyes, Daria's stepsister flounced toward the door in a cloud of lavender perfume. "Don't be an idiot, Daria. I'm *borrowing* the outfit. There's a difference." She twisted her lips. "We're family, and family lends their possessions to each other."

"Right. Because you and Magnolia are so generous with your things." Daria crossed her arms. "And you'd be happy to loan me your green hat." Not that she actually wanted to be seen in the confection of feathers, ribbons, and netting, but the satisfaction of watching Pansy's face tighten was worth an afternoon of discomfort.

"It's not your style. You don't have the panache to wear one of Mrs. Hogan's creations, but I'm sure I can find something in my closet that's suited to you." Pansy looked down her nose. "Besides, you have chores to complete. Mother has already said you can't go to the party if you don't finish your tasks. As Benjamin Franklin said, 'It is the working man who is the happy man. It is the idle man who is the miserable man.'"

Daria laughed. "He also said, 'Tricks and treachery are the practice of fools, that don't have brains enough to be honest.'"

With a squeal, Pansy grabbed the crystal vase from the nearby table and flung it across the room.

"No!" Daria ducked, and the urn crashed on the tile floor and shattered. "That was a gift from my father. How dare you break it." She ran to her stepsister and shoved her against the wall, hand itching to slap the girl who constantly belittled and bullied her.

The door opened with a bang. Her stepmother, Amaryllis, glared at them from the threshold. "What on earth is going on in here? Alley cats make less noise." Her gaze slid to the scattered shards of glass, then back to Daria. "What did you do? That piece was worth a lot of money."

"Your daughter threw it at me during a temper tantrum." Daria's lip curled. "And its monetary value is of no concern to you. Father gave it to me for my sixteenth birthday."

Like the great horned owl that prowled the forest outside the house, Amaryllis's neck swiveled, and she pierced Daria with a dark look.

"Pansy does not tend toward hysterics. Don't blame others for your own sins."

Pansy lifted her chin and smirked. "Yeah, don't try to get me into trouble for your bad behaviors."

"You lying—"

"Stop!" Amaryllis held up her hand. "I've had enough of your attitude, Daria. You act as if you are better than my daughters and me. I've tried to guide you into adulthood, teaching you skills that will do you well as a wife and mother, but you've thwarted me at every turn. I'm done with you. You will remain in your room for the rest of the night, thinking about how you can change to become a contributing member of this family."

"Contributing member? I do more in a day than both your daughters do in a year."

"You go on thinking that, my dear." Amaryllis pointed to the broken vase. "Especially while you're cleaning up the heirloom you seem to care about so much."

"What about the garden party this afternoon?" Daria frowned. "I've been invited to attend, as have you three."

"You should have thought of that before breaking the vase."

"But I didn't break it."

Amaryllis pressed a hand to her chest. "Your father would be heartbroken to see you now. God rest his soul."

"Don't bring Father into this. He was a good and decent man." Daria's voice wavered, and she cleared her throat. "How you managed to pull the wool over his eyes about your true nature is beyond me. Perhaps love really is blind."

"I will not have you disrespect me in this manner." Amaryllis drew herself to her full height. "Come, Pansy, we've got a party to prepare for." She pointed at Daria. "And you will stay in here for a week on bread and water. Hopefully, that will be sufficient time for you to consider the consequences of your actions."

"I'm just as happy not to attend a gathering filled with pretentious and disingenuous people like you. The servants are better company."

With a glare, Amaryllis and Pansy left the room, and the door slammed, the key clicking in the lock.

An hour later, Daria had swept the remains of Father's gift into the trash bin, then sat staring out the window at the birds playing in the air currents in the sky. Ah, to have such freedom. Movement below caught her attention, and she gaped at her stepmother and stepsisters leaving the house, each wearing one of her mother's gowns. She thought Father had disposed of the dresses long ago.

She bit her lip to keep from crying out. To let them see her anguish would only give them satisfaction. They'd obviously been planning her banishment for a while. Amaryllis knew she'd object to their wearing of Mother's dresses. Heatedly. So she'd probably arranged the altercation with Pansy.

Daria huffed out a breath, tears welling in her eyes. She'd fallen into their trap. *Oh, Father, why did you have to marry Amaryllis, then die?*

The carriage wheels crunched on the stone as it rolled out of the driveway. Moments later, the conveyance turned onto the lane leading to town, then disappeared behind the trees.

Dear Lord, please help me.

Hinges squeaking, the door swung open. Rosamunde, the elderly servant who'd come with Mother when she married Father, marched into the room, a newspaper in hand and her face set in a scowl. "You need to flee, and I've got just the thing."

Daria stared at her. "Flee? Where? How?"

Rosamunde spread the publication onto the table, then flipped several pages. Her fingers ran down the columns, her lips moving as she read silently. "Here they are. Look."

"What?" Daria stood next to the woman and peered at the paper. "Matrimonial news? I don't understand."

"These are advertisements for mail-order brides. There are hundreds...maybe thousands of men out West who are lonely. They put advertisements in the Eastern newspapers for wives. Read the ads. Select one or more and reply." Rosamunde smiled. "Life will not improve here, only worsen. You need to go, and the sooner the better."

"But to marry a man I've never met. What if I'm exchanging one nightmare for another?"

"You can use an agency." Rosamunde pointed to a bold-faced announcement. "Look at this. Westward Home and Hearts Matrimonial Agency, Millie Crenshaw, proprietress. Run by a woman. That sounds promising. Contact her. You have nothing to lose."

"You're right, Rosamunde. Thank you for helping me." Daria hugged the elderly woman. "You could get fired if Amaryllis finds out about this."

"I've got me a little nest egg. Been saving for years. Always planned to leave once you were grown and out on your own. Now is as good a time as any." She winked. "And I like to see how they fare without me."

Daria giggled. "Not well, I would imagine." She sucked in a deep breath. "Okay, I'll contact the agency. Millie is a nice name. Hopefully, she is a nice lady." Her chin trembled. "Do you know the worst of it, Rosamunde?"

"What, honey?"

"Today is the anniversary of Father's death. He's been gone ten years exactly, and not one of them seems to remember."

"All the more reason for you to go, sweetheart."

Rocky Mountain Springs, WY

Chapter Two

Laughter punctuated the buzz of conversation as Ewan McKay sauntered along the tables in the churchyard and filled his plate. Winter had finally loosened its grip on the tiny community, allowing the monthly potluck to be held outside. A warm breeze smelling of fresh cut grass stroked his cheeks and tugged at his Stetson.

Children raced around the grassy meadow, their shrieks splitting the air. Women had exchanged their somber wool dresses for pastel and sprigged muslin. Men had shed their leather jackets.

A year had passed since his arrival, not nearly enough time to acclimate to the long, snowy season that had lasted for six months. Before coming, he'd heard about the vastness of America but hadn't truly believed the stories until chugging along the rails for two weeks. The Wyoming mountains made Ben Nevis in the Scottish Highlands seem like an anthill. There were days he missed the Old Country, but not enough to return.

Ewan reached the end of the smorgasbord and turned to find somewhere to sit. Several yards away, Rayne Wade waved and pointed to a seat next to her. Her red hair glistened in the sun, and her green eyes sparkled. Her husband, Flynn, was a lucky man. Not only was she a beautiful woman, but she was intelligent, witty, and gracious. She'd played a large part in helping Ewan integrate into the small town.

He hurried to their table and lowered himself on the bench, then set down his plate. "You ladies have outdone yourselves this month. I'm not sure I can eat all I've chosen."

Rayne snickered and nudged his shoulder. "You say that at every potluck, yet always manage to clean your plate."

Chuckling, Ewan took a swig of water. "I hate to disappoint anyone."

Flynn forked a piece of chicken. "You're just happy to have someone else do your cooking."

"I won't deny that." Ewan shrugged. "If I lived closer to town, I'd probably eat at the diner every day." Movement caught his eye. He looked up, and his lips thinned. Hair swept into an ornate style and wearing a pink silk dress, Hilda Jenkins glided past on the arm of a man he'd never seen before. Obviously well-off, her companion wore a close-fitting, charcoal-colored frock coat. His vest sported intricate embroidery with the gold chain of his pocket watch spanning his trim torso. The trousers appeared to be gray Angola.

"Pay her no mind." Rayne sniffed. "She's just trying to get your goat."

"It's working." Ewan plowed a carrot chunk through his mashed potatoes. "I should be relieved that I discovered what sort of woman she is before our wedding, but I feel the perfect fool for not seeing her true colors."

"She's a social climber. I saw my fair share of those in Portland." She shuddered. "Can you imagine if she'd received the letter about your father after you'd married?"

"My father's situation shouldn't have any bearing on my life here. Aren't you American women supposed to be less pretentious than those in the United Kingdom. Besides, the charges are fraudulent. I just have to figure out how to prove his innocence."

"Hilda's cousins live in Britain, so she's traveled abroad and apparently took a liking to the gentry." Rayne shook her head. "It's a shame you haven't taken a shine to any of the other single women in Rocky Mountain Springs."

"There are but a few, and I've tried to see them as potential wives, but it's no use. I feel nothing for any of them." He cocked his head. "Am I being unrealistic in expecting to have a marriage like my mum and da who loved each other dearly?"

"Absolutely not!" Rayne bolted upright. "God wants His children to have loving and happy marriages."

Ewan laid down his fork and pushed away the half-filled plate, his meal sitting like a stone in his stomach. "Then He better figure out how to provide a wife in the middle of nowhere."

Flynn grinned and crossed his arms. "He already has. Don't you remember that Rayne and I found each other through the mail? I certainly never expected that. Perhaps God will use the postal system to give you a wife."

"I dinnae..."

"It worked for Flynn and me. Maybe you should consider using the Westward Home and Hearts Matrimonial Agency. Millie Crenshaw is a genius at pairing men and women." Rayne gazed at her husband, her face aglow. "From your expression, I can tell you're skeptical, but it can, and does, work. Flynn and I love each other." Her cheeks pinked. "Very much."

Ewan patted her hand. "I know you do, Rayne. And Flynn is lucky to have found you."

"But that's just it." Flynn leaned forward. "Luck had nothing to do with it. I firmly believe God led her to me. Not that he condoned her impersonating her sister, but He allowed events to happen so we'd meet." He twisted his lips. "I'm no scholar, and I'm not sure how sound my theology is, but I feel that He handpicked her for me. He can do the same for you if you ask Him."

"My prayer life has suffered since the situation with Hilda." Ewan's face warmed. "I blamed God rather than considering how things worked out to be a blessing." He rubbed at a worn spot on the table. "Guess I need to take your suggestion to heart...and to the Lord."

Rayne wrapped one arm around his shoulder in a quick hug. "That's wonderful, Ewan. And Flynn and I will pray for a resolution as well.

"You think this Millie person can really find a woman who doesnae put on airs and is willing to marry a lowly law clerk?"

"I'll bet God is preparing your wife this very minute."

Ewan rubbed the back of his neck. But was he prepared?

Chapter Three

Scenery outside the glass blurred in a mixture of green, brown, and blue. Daria clutched her reticule and closed her eyes, her stomach protesting against the constant swaying of the train. Fortunately, her intended groom had wired enough money for her to travel second class, so she wasn't crammed shoulder to shoulder on a hard bench in third class. Not quite as luxurious as the décor she'd glimpsed in first class, but comfortable.

Somewhere behind her a baby gurgled, and Daria sighed. Thanks to help from Rosamunde, she'd obtained the freedom she yearned for. A telegram to the matrimonial agency had resulted in a visit from Millie Crenshaw herself. The woman had been visiting Newport, which the servant had insisted was a sign from God. Daria wasn't so sure, but she wouldn't scoff at her good fortune.

Amaryllis had been most unhappy at the turn of events, her face twisted as if she'd bitten into a lemon. But with a few pointed words, Miss

Crenshaw had reminded her stepmother that Daria was of age and did not need permission to apply as a mail-order bride, or Amaryllis's presence in the interview. The proprietress had been gracious and understanding, assuring Daria she was the perfect candidate for the agency, and that she would depart immediately.

A smile tugged at her lips at the memory of peeking out the back window of the carriage and seeing her stepmother and stepsisters gape at the well-appointed conveyance as it rolled away. Against Daria's protestations, Miss Crenshaw had arranged for her to stay at the same hotel until final plans could be made for a husband.

Two days later, news arrived that she would become the bride of a Scottish man living in Wyoming. Excitement had warred with terror and continued to do so with each turn of the wheel. Details about her groom-to-be were sparse other than the facts that he was two years older than her and a recent immigrant to America, having left his homeland last year.

He was a believer, but would his faith resemble hers? What would it be like to be wed to a foreigner? Were his expectations of a wife different than those of an American man? Did she know how to be a wife? She could cook and clean. Amaryllis had made sure of that when she'd relegated her to the status of a servant, but what about entertaining? A wave of nausea swept over her, and she swallowed.

"Miss? Are you ill?"

Daria's eyes flew open, and she turned to the voice.

A man of perhaps thirty years old stood in the aisle, concern etched on his face. "I'm Dr. Flint Nolan. How may I help you?"

Her cheeks warmed. "I...uh...no...it's nerves. That's all."

He gestured to the vacant seat beside her. "May I?"

Pulling her skirts close, she nodded. "I feel rather foolish that you noticed my discomfort."

"As a physician, I have the unfortunate habit of watching people. I doubt anyone else saw your distress." He laced his fingers. "I don't want to pry, but do you care to share the source of your uneasiness?"

She studied his face and sensed no trace of duplicity. Could she trust this man? Was he a doctor as he claimed?

His smile faltered. "If I've offended you..."

"No." She shrugged. "Not at all."

"I'm being too forward." His forehead creased, and he rose. "My sister warned me that my lack of manners would get me in trouble one day."

"Please, sit." She tugged his sleeve. "You've not been forward, and I appreciate your care."

He resumed his seat.

"I'm going to Rocky Mountain Springs to marry, and I'm a bit anxious. We'll be there soon, and I'm not sure I'm ready."

"Rocky Mountains Springs is my destination, too. How fortuitous to meet you." He cocked his head. "Are you one of those mail-order brides I've heard about?"

"Yes, so I've not met my husband-to-be."

"Haven't you corresponded? I thought that's how it worked."

Daria nibbled her lower lip. "Most times, or so I've been told, but I came out of a...uh...difficult situation, so I used an agency to make the arrangements. Things were handled rather quickly."

"Ah." Dr. Nolan crossed his arms. "Well, truth be told, I'm a tad nervous myself. I'm going to be the new doctor in town."

"That's wonderful." Tension slipped from her shoulders. "It's nice to be where there are medical facilities. I know nothing about Wyoming and imagine it to be very wild."

"But getting tamer by the month. One of the reasons I'm willing to have my children join me after I get settled."

She reared back. "Oh. You're married?"

His shoulders sagged. "No. Well, I was. I lost my wife six months ago in childbirth."

Her eyes filled with tears. "I'm sorry."

Dr. Nolan blinked and cleared his throat. "Thank you. I'm looking forward to a fresh start in Rocky Mountain Springs."

"As am I." She held out her hand. "And now we each know one person in town."

He shook her hand and chuckled. "Yes, we do."

"Next stop, Rocky Mountain Springs!" The porter strolled down the aisle. "Rocky Mountain Springs, next stop."

Daria pressed her hand against her stomach. "Well, ready or not, we're here."

Thirty minutes later, the brakes squealed, and the train lurched to a stop. Dr. Flint stepped into the aisle and crooked his arm. "Let me assist you onto the platform."

She slipped her hand through his elbow, and they made their way out of the train. A family of five, two men, and a couple also disembarked. A short distance away, a medium-built man with dark hair stood near a wagon, his eyes riveted on the locomotive. His gaze shot from her to Dr. Nolan, and he frowned.

"Mr. McKay?" Daria extricated her hand from Dr. Nolan's arm and held out her hand.

"Aye." He scowled and glared at Dr. Nolan as if the man was a leper. "Miss Burke?"

"Yes." Her heart pounded in her chest. Why was her groom-to-be so surly? "It's nice to meet you. This is Dr. Nolan. He's the town's new doctor. We met by accident on the train."

"I'll bet." He lifted an eyebrow, then glanced toward the stack of trunks and satchels the porters pulled from the baggage car and piled on the platform. "One of those yours?"

She turned and dipped her head to the doctor. "Thank you for your assistance. I hope to see you again."

He bowed, then looked at Mr. McKay and touched the brim of his hat. "Good day, sir."

"Nolan." Her intended pivoted and marched toward the stack of luggage. "Let's go."

Daria gaped at his departing figure, then hurried to catch up with him. In the span of two minutes, her fiancé was rude and dictatorial. Had she made the biggest mistake of her life?

Jaw thrust forward, Ewan gestured toward the tower of bags. "Which ones are yours?" He winced at the censure in his voice, but he had a right to be upset. She'd disembarked on the arm of some dandy.

Miss Burke's forehead creased, and she pointed to a small black trunk that had seen better days. He knew from the matrimonial agency she had fallen on hard times after the death of her father. When had the man died? Had the lack of a male figure in her life created loose morals? Why else would she think it acceptable to attach herself to a perfect stranger?

He picked up the chest and hefted it onto his shoulder. Not as heavy as he thought it would be. Jerking his head toward the wagon, he said, "That's us. I can help you up after I stow your luggage."

"No, thank you." She lifted her skirts and climbed into the conveyance, with the grace of a roe deer cresting a Highland hill. She sat down and tucked her skirt under her legs. Ramrod straight, she stared straight ahead.

With quick motions, he stashed her possessions, jumped into the wagon, and lowered himself beside her. His shoulder bumped hers, and a tingle shot across his back. His eyes widened, and he grabbed the reins. "We havenae had a chance to discuss the arrangement. Did Miss Crenshaw explain that you'll be staying in the hotel here in town until we decide when we'll marry?" *If* he married her. He'd wait until he determined her true nature.

"She informed me." She spoke through stiff lips and didn't look at him. "I'd be happy to pay for my lodging, an expense I'm sure you didn't expect to incur."

"No! I mean, I'll take care of the charges. I've asked you to come. It's only fair that I pay."

"All right." She plucked at her skirt, then laced her fingers. "Miss Crenshaw told me you are a lawyer. I don't expect you to entertain me during working hours. I can find things to do, but I hope that we will have some time to get acquainted."

"I have to work each day, but Mr. Ilbert has agreed to reduce my hours for the next few weeks to allow us time together. That way we can determine if we're suited to each other."

Her chin lifted, and a steely glint came into her eyes. "You're concerned we're not?"

He hesitated as he pulled on the right trace to steer the horse perpendicular to the walkway in front of the hotel. "Whoa." The wagon came to a stop, but he remained seated. "We know nothing about each other. As much as I'd like a wife, Miss Burke, I'm hesitant to commit to someone I've just met. Someone who seems...uh...overly social."

"I beg your pardon?" Her spine stiffened. "What on earth do you mean by that?"

"Dr. Nolan." He licked his lips. "You exited the train on the man's arm. How much time did you spend with him during the journey?"

She jumped to her feet, her face flushed. "How dare you suggest I acted inappropriately with the doctor." She spoke through gritted teeth. "I met him a mere thirty minutes before we arrived, and he was gracious enough to help me off the train so I didn't fall and injure myself. As any *gentleman* would. But perhaps you wouldn't know about that." Her chin trembled, and she pressed her lips together.

"I just—"

"I believe I'm quite fatigued after my trip, Mr. McKay. I'll be inside, if you'd be so kind as to bring in my luggage." She climbed out of the wagon and marched into the hotel, head held high.

He blew out a deep breath. Had he just ruined his last chance to find a wife?

Chapter Four

Heart pounding, Daria entered the hotel and froze. She was definitely not in Newport anymore. Scuffed wooden floors and whitewashed walls surrounded her. The windows featured white cotton curtains, and the upholstered furniture was mismatched. Although plain, the room was clean and tidy. A young man of perhaps her age smiled at her from behind a tall wooden counter. If Mr. McKay saw her talking to the clerk would he exhibit the same jealous behavior?

She swallowed a sigh and approached the reception desk. "I'm Daria Burke. There should be a reservation for me."

"Welcome to Rocky Mountain Springs, miss. You are in room five upstairs." He glanced behind her. "Do you have any luggage?"

Just then, the door opened with a bang, and Mr. McKay strode into the lobby, her trunk on his shoulder. The scowl on his face had been replaced by an impassive mask.

"Ah, Mr. McKay. Nice to see you. If you leave the trunk over here, the porter will see that it gets to Miss Burke's room." The clerk gestured a spot next to the counter. "Will you be joining us for dinner this evening?"

"Aye." Mr. McKay set down the chest as if is weighed little more than a book. He looked at her. "Will five o'clock be acceptable to you, Miss Burke?"

"Yes, that will be fine." She licked her dry lips. Would they ever get past the awkwardness?

He bowed, then pivoted and hurried out the door.

As the clerk handed her a key dangling from a thin chain, a lanky, freckle-faced boy bounded across the lobby. He picked up her case with surprising ease, then headed for the stairs.

"Is there anything else I can do for you, Miss Burke?"

After the interaction with Mr. McKay, she almost wept at the kindness in the man's voice. "No, thank you."

"If you change your mind, please don't hesitate to ask. Enjoy your stay."

With a nod, she trudged to the stairs and ascended to the second floor. The porter waited by an open door. "You're in here, miss. The pitcher has been filled with fresh water, and towels are in the top drawer. Maid service is performed twice per week."

She dug into her reticule and pressed a coin into the young man's palm. "It's lovely. Thank you for your help."

"Any time, miss." He blushed and hurried down the stairs, his clomping bootsteps fading.

Like the lobby, the room was plain, but clean and tidy. A pine four-poster bed took up most of the space, flanked by pine nightstands. An armoire and bureau took up the wall at the end of the bed with a full-length mirror tucked in one corner. A blue-and-yellow patchwork quilt covered the bed. The window was covered with the same white cotton curtains used downstairs. Although a far cry from Newport luxury, the room was perfect. Just the fresh start she needed.

Ignoring the trunk, she stretched out on the mattress and closed her eyes. She could unpack in a bit. For now, she'd rest her weary body and consider her situation.

Mr. McKay was attractive. She'd give him that. Not quite as tall as her father's six-foot frame, he had broad, muscular shoulders. Wide-set blue eyes were set deep in his tanned face under a head of thick, dark-brown hair that curled slightly on his collar. His jaw was square, his lips full. Would she ever see them curved into a smile?

Why did Miss Crenshaw think he would make Daria a good husband? Thus far, he'd been anything but warm and welcoming. He'd apparently deceived the agency owner as to his true nature, and he was too much like Amaryllis for Daria's liking.

"What should I do?" She sat up and rubbed the back of her neck. "I'd rather be alone and penniless than married to someone who will crush me under his thumb. I can't exchange one bully for another. I won't!"

She swung her feet over the side of the bed. "I should contact Miss Crenshaw. Tell her this won't work." Daria twisted her lips. "But will she try to find me someone else, or is it this man or no one?" They hadn't talked much about what to do if either she or Mr. McKay found the situation untenable.

Her stomach fluttered, and she pressed her hand against her middle. "No time for nerves, Daria. First things first, send a telegram to the agency to determine how to proceed. Hopefully, she'd have an answer by morning, but if not, she'd tough it out with the man. She'd suffered under her stepmother's hand for years. She could handle a few days with an arrogant, grumpy man. For the present, she had a place to stay and was safe from Amaryllis, and that's all that mattered.

Rising, she smoothed her skirts and went to the mirror where she inspected her appearance. Pale from fatigue, but otherwise presentable. "Now to find out when the next train leaves Rocky Mountain Springs and where it goes. I'm not going to trade one cruel person for another. Not when I've finally gained my freedom."

An image of Dr. Nolan came to mind. Would he hire her as an assistant? No. She didn't have any experience in medicine. But he'd been so solicitous. Should she seek his advice? No. Doing so might put him in a difficult position. But she had not doubt he'd help her if asked. She'd save that possibility as a last resort.

"All right, Daria. Determine your options, then you can make your plans." She straightened her spine, pinned a smile on her face, and left the room. She descended to the lobby.

The clerk leapt to his feet behind the desk. "Miss Burke, is everything okay?"

"Yes. The room is lovely." She leaned toward him. "I'm hoping you can give me some information about the train schedule?"

His forehead creased. "But you've only just arrived."

"Considering running out already?"

Daria whirled, and her stomach clenched.

Hat in hand, Mr. McKay stood in the middle of the lobby, the ever-present scowl darkening his face.

Chapter Five

"You're leaving?" Ewan's hands tightened on his hat. Miss Burke had been in Wyoming less than two hours, and she'd already changed her mind about marrying him. Would he ever find happiness with a woman? "Were you going to tell me or simply disappear?"

Her cheeks reddened, but she lifted her chin, and her face held a cool expression. "Do you really want to have this conversation here? In the lobby?" She rolled her eyes toward the clerk, who was watching them with fascination.

"No, of course not." He glanced around the room, then gestured to a pair of Chippendale-style upholstered chairs nestled in one corner. "Will you join me over there?"

"Certainly." She pulled her skirts close and marched to the alcove, then lowered herself on one of the seats. She crossed her ankles and laced her fingers in her lap.

He sat in the other vacant chair and laid his hat on his knee, then swept the room with his gaze. The desk clerk had returned to his business, and the only other people in the lobby were two men deep in conversation. Good. He turned his attention back to Miss Burke to find her studying him, one eyebrow raised. She was no shrinking violet. Was that a gift or a curse? He cleared his throat. "I'll ask you again: are you leaving Rocky Mountain Springs?"

"To be honest, I haven't decided. After getting settled in my room, I found myself replaying the events that happened as I arrived. You've been alternately surly and noncommunicative since the moment I stepped off the train. I suffered long enough under those behaviors." Her shoulders sagged. "A woman alone has few options, but I will make my own way if necessary."

"I'm sorry." Ewan pursed his lips. "You're correct that I've been beastly. When I saw you on the arm of that Nolan man, I imagined the worst. Then to find out he was a doctor, well..." He fiddled with the brim of his hat. "I thought I was getting rejected again because I'm not well-off or important."

"Dr. Nolan was escorting me." She narrowed her eyes. "How could you equate that with my refusing you?"

"It was *glaikit*...foolish. I allowed my pride to get the best of me." He licked his lips. "Will you stay and give me, give us, a chance?"

A long moment passed, and his stomach churned. He'd lost Hilda through no fault of his own, but the blunder of the bonny Miss Burke walking out on him could only be laid at his feet.

"All right." She gave him a tentative smile. "But there are going to be a few ground rules."

His breath whooshed out of him, and he straightened. "Whatever you say. Again, I apologize for my boorish behavior. It's not who I am. I promise."

"That remains to be seen." She cocked her head. "Honesty is important to me. We cannot have a true relationship if we keep our thoughts and feelings to ourselves. When you are upset, please tell me. I cannot fix what I don't know is broken."

"I agree. Let's begin again." He stuck out his hand. "Thank you for answering my advertisement and your willingness to consider me as a husband, Miss Burke. I look forward to getting acquainted."

Her face suffused with a delightful shade of pink, and she grasped his fingers for a few seconds. "As do I."

A tingle shot from his palm to his elbow, and his eyes widened. He cleared his throat. "Would you mind terribly if we used our given names? Miss Burke and Mr. McKay seem so formal. Especially out here in the *Wild West*."

"I would be pleased to use our names." She giggled. "Is the area truly as wild as it's purported to be?"

He grinned. "Perhaps not as much as in the early days, but there are occasional incidents, and it's not Edinburgh or Glasgow, that's for sure. But I will keep you safe."

"Thank you."

Ewan's chest swelled. Her smile made him feel like both a schoolboy and Robert the Bruce. "I'm glad we've made amends."

"Me, too. Why are you here? We agreed to meet for dinner."

He blinked. He'd been so flabbergasted to hear her ask about the train schedule, the reason for his visit had flown completely from his mind. "I came to ask you a favor, but you are welcome to say no."

"I'd be happy to help in any way I can."

"As you know, I am apprenticing for an attorney, and our secretary has up and quit to seek his fortune in the Dakota Territory. Word has reached town of another gold rush. Miss Crenshaw said that you were bright and well-educated. I told Mr. Ilbert, and he'd like to meet you."

"Secretary? At a law firm?" An expression of wonder bloomed on her face. "I don't know..."

"Please? Come and meet Mr. Ilbert. He's a bit gruff, but he's a good man. Frankly, I was surprised when he said he'd consider using you, but we're desperate." He wiped his palms on his pants. "I think you'd be wonderful."

She grinned. "Are you saying that so I'll take the job?"

He chuckled. "No. I've already determined there's no pulling the wool over your eyes, and you dinnae back down. Two good characteristics at a law firm. We get all kinds. You would make a great addition to the office."

Jumping to her feet, she patted her hair. "Then let's get to it, shall we?"

"Aye." He clamped on his hat. "Dinnae you need time to prepare?"

"Hardly. I'll retrieve my hat and reticule." Her lips twisted in an uncertain smile. "Unless you think I should change my clothing..."

"Nonsense. You look lovely."

"I won't be but a moment." She hurried across the lobby, her skirts rustling as she walked.

He watched as she ascended the stairs, then turned to the window and scrubbed at his face with cold fingers. He'd nearly lost her, and something told him that would have been a tragedy. Would Mr. Ilbert accept her? Working together every day would be the perfect opportunity to see who Miss Burke, nay, Daria, really was. Daria. The name felt good rolling off his lips.

"I'm ready."

He startled and whirled. "That was fast."

"You said time was of the essence."

"I did, but most women dinnae get ready so quickly."

"I'm not most women."

He winked and crooked his arm. "I'm beginning to see that."

Chapter Six

Dust swirled around her skirts as Daria followed Ewan to his office. Harnesses jingled, wagons rattled, and horses whinnied. Conversation mingled with laughter and shouts. Everywhere she looked were men. Tall, short, beefy, skinny, well-dressed, and unkempt. The bulk were white, but the occasional dark face appeared among the pedestrians. Even fewer were women.

A swarthy man with a bushy beard leered at her as they passed. She shuddered and drew closer to Mr. McKay...Ewan. An unusual name, but she liked it. Yew-en. She'd ask him later what it meant.

They arrived in front of a glossy black door. Gilt letters on the glass touted: Jacob Ilbert, Attorney at Law.

Ewan turned the knob and opened the door, then gestured for her to enter.

She stepped inside, and her eyebrows shot up. Two massive wooden desks, oak if she wasn't mistaken, faced each other in the center of the room. On one wall, a matching bookshelf was packed with leather-bound volumes. A tiny stove and sink were against another wall. Standing in the threshold of a doorway on the far side of the room was a short, balding man. Piercing brown eyes watched her through gold wire-rim glasses perched on his nose. She had no doubt he was a formidable force in the courtroom.

Heart pounding, she curtsied, not something she normally did, but it seemed best to acknowledge the man's importance.

He walked toward her, a slight limp to his gait. "You must be Miss Burke. Thank you for coming. Does that mean you're willing to help us?"

"Yes, sir." She dipped her head. "I can start right away."

His gaze raked her face. "Quite unorthodox, you know, having a woman as a secretary." He shrugged. "But it can't be helped. Mr. McKay seems to think you're capable of the work."

"I understand."

"Worst case you'll be a dismal failure, but your presence will give us time to find someone more appropriate."

Daria straightened her spine and lifted her chin to meet his stare. "I assure you that I'm up to the task. If you'll outline my responsibilities, I can get started."

"That remains to be seen, but we're desperate." He scratched his jaw. "You will copy various documents, some on the typewriter, others by hand." His lips twisted. "I hope your penmanship is acceptable. You will keep the files current, and the supplies stocked, such as paper, ink, and the like. Think you can handle those chores?"

"Absolutely."

"Good. Keeping the office clean and the coffee made will also fall on you. Occasionally, we will work long hours, and you will bring us meals. Do you have any problems with that?"

"Not at all. Whatever it takes to help you get your work done."

He crossed his arms and peered down his nose at her. "Be aware that you may see or hear shocking things. Things no woman should be privy to, but every scrap of information that goes through this office is confidential. Women have a tendency to gossip, so you need to refrain from the urge to do so."

She clenched her fists. What a misogynist. If he was married, she felt sorry for his wife. "I have neither the inclination nor the time to carry tales, Mr. Ilbert." She spoke through wooden lips. "And frankly, men can be just as loose-lipped. Now, if that's everything you need to tell me, I'll get to work."

Beside her, Ewan drew in a breath, but Mr. Ilbert chuckled. "You're right, McKay. She won't take hogwash from anyone. Familiarize her with our cases, then take her to the courthouse and file that appeal. Welcome aboard, Miss Burke." He withdrew into his office and closed the door.

Ewan squeezed her shoulder. "Well done, lass. He's not an easy man to impress."

"That's not what I set out to do."

He grinned. "Which is why you did. I see too many obsequious people try to ingratiate themselves to him. He has no patience for those behaviors."

She shrugged, then surveyed the room. Her knees quivered, and she put a hand on the wall to steady herself. Whether the man was impressed or not meant little, however the handsome Scotsman was another story. Despite their inauspicious beginning, she didn't want to be a disappointment to him.

"You'll do fine." Ewan swallowed a grin. She'd do more than fine with the amount of grit and gumption she'd exhibited. Firm in responding to Mr. Ilbert's less-than-veiled insult about women, she'd held her own. He gestured to the desk with the typewriter. "This is where you'll sit. Have you ever used one of these machines? Very few businesses have them, but Mr. Ilbert sees them as the wave of the future."

"No, but I will do my best to learn." She ran her fingers along the roller, then pressed one of the letters. A metal bar rose from within the machine. "How clever."

"Aye, but most people dinnae trust the idea of mechanical writing, especially signatures."

"Remington?" She pointed to the name on the front of the machine. "I thought they manufactured guns."

"They did, and still do. However, after the war they wanted to be known for more than weapons, but their foray into these machines has only been recent."

"Very savvy. It will be interesting to see how they fare."

Ewan dragged the chair from her desk next to his. "Let's review the cases, then we'll head to the courthouse."

She sat down, and her arm brushed his. A tremor raced up his shoulder at her touch. Did she feel that? He cleared his throat and drew the stack of papers toward them. As he leafed through the sheets, he explained the reason for each and outlined the associated cases.

Her questions were razor-sharp and spot on. If women were ever allowed to practice law, Daria would make a fine attorney. He blinked. Where had that thought come from? He'd known her less than a handful of hours. "In addition to paying clients, Mr. Ilbert takes on a limited number of pro bono cases. Uh...free."

"Shortened from the phrase pro bono publico, meaning for the public good."

He cocked his head. "You're schooled in Latin?"

"Not fully, but my father was a voracious reader, and he believed in educating women. I had access to his library, and he would assign me certain things to read, then discuss them." Grief colored her voice, and moisture glistened in her eyes. "He loved the early philosophers."

"He sounds like a remarkable man." He patted her hand. "I would like to hear more about him sometime."

Nodding, she sniffled. "And I would like to tell you, but for now we have work to do."

"You're a worse taskmaster than Mr. Ilbert." He winked. "He's going to admire you."

Daria giggled, then blinked away her tears. "Do many lawyers help people without money?"

"I'm not sure. I dinnae see much of that in Scotland, and I've only worked for Mr. Ilbert here in America. I would hope so. The poor need as much help as the rich in navigating the court system."

Her lips thinned. "Sometimes more."

"Aye." He studied her. Had she been wronged by the courts? Now was not the time, but he would explore her past experiences. "The pro bono cases are our most satisfying. At least, to me. Ofttimes, the dispute involves the needy being taken advantage of by a landlord or other person of power over them. Sadly, most people in the lower classes are afraid to do anything about the situation, so I'm pleased when we can help even a few. We hope that word will get out about our willingness to represent them."

She smiled at him, her eyes glowing. "It's wonderful to see you so passionate about helping the less fortunate."

His chest swelled. How could her assessment affect him after mere hours together? Had his loneliness for companionship made him susceptible to any kindness from a female, or could he possibly be attracted to her already?

Chapter Seven

Finished with the housekeeping chores, Daria poured a cup of coffee and took it into Mr. Ilbert's office. She set the mug on the corner of his desk with a quiet thunk, then stepped back and clasped her hands in front of her.

He pulled out his pocket watch, popped it open, and nodded. "Right on time as usual, Miss Burke. Thank you." He took a sip of the dark brew. "I'm pleased with the progress you've made after only two days. We've had an old case resurface. Mr. McKay will require your help in comparing the files with the new evidence. I'd like a report by the end of the week outlining the discrepancies."

"Yes, sir. Will there be anything else? Something to eat perhaps? I could run to the diner."

"No, but I won't have time for a lunch break, so have something delivered at noon. You and Mr. McKay will want to work through your meal as well."

"Of course, sir." She turned and tiptoed from the room. The attorney wasn't exactly warm and friendly, but he treated her with respect. And compliments were few and far between, so to receive one brought a smile to her lips.

She closed the door and slipped into the chair at her desk. Ewan looked up, his habit of finger-combing his thick sable-colored hair evident by the spikes on his head. Her heart thundered against her ribs. Did he know how devastatingly handsome he was?

His blue eyes twinkled. "Taking the boss's coffee to him on a schedule is a brilliant move. He feels quite the king."

"He *does* own the practice."

"That he does." He laid down his pen. "But your attention to minute details hasn't gone unnoticed. You've already put our last secretary to shame with the amount of work you complete in a fraction of the time."

Her face warmed. Ewan's words meant more to her than Mr. Ilbert's. "I appreciate being given a chance to assist you. I've enjoyed the challenge and have learned a tremendous amount in the two days I've been here." She leaned forward. "Did he tell you that I'm to assist you on a case that has been reopened?"

"Aye." Ewan cocked his head. "You seem eager, but the job will be tedious, going through mountains of paperwork and comparing line after line of testimony, notes, and the like. Life in a law office isnae as exciting as one would think."

"I'll take monotony over drama any day of the week." She tucked a stray hair behind her ear. "How would you like to split the task?"

"Two of the witnesses have recanted their testimony, and a new witness has come forward. There are other issues as well, but we'll start with the original statements."

Daria opened a drawer and retrieved several sheets of paper. "I'll make a chart that compares their assertions."

"Perfect."

With a few quick motions, she drew lines on the paper and labeled the columns. "Ready." She looked up, and her pulse tripped. His crystal-blue eyes were riveted on her. His proximity was distracting enough, but to find him staring turned her mind to mashed potatoes. Moisture sprang to her palms, and she wiped her hands on her skirts. Focus, girl!

He blinked and cleared his throat, then began to read from his notes.

Her pen raced over the pages as she captured the material. An hour passed. Then two. The muscles in her back screamed from sitting in one position for so long, but she ignored the pain. If he could remain in his chair, she would too.

Periodically, he'd give her one of the sheets and ask for help deciphering the scrawl. Their hands would graze, and a jolt like nothing she'd ever felt would shoot up her arm. Could he feel the tingles?

Ink-stained, his long, tapered fingers flew over the papers as he sifted through the records. His expression, a combination of doggedness and enthusiasm, showed his passion for ferreting out the truth. His intelligence was evident as he analyzed the information, cutting through superfluous words.

He'd sought her opinion twice since her employment began, the difficulties of their initial meeting a distant memory. Father had always told her first impressions were important, but apparently second impressions counted for something, too.

Squelching the desire to smooth his hair, she fiddled with her necklace, a locket that had belonged to her mother. *Oh, Mama, why did you and Father have to die? I could use your advice. Ewan seems like a good man, but marriage is forever. How do I know he's the man for me? Should I ask him to help me with Father's estate? To regain that which is rightfully mine? Or should I remain in obscurity?*

"Miss Burke? Daria?" Concern creased Ewan's forehead. "Is everything all right?"

She released the necklace. "Yes. I'm sorry. Carry on." She dropped her gaze and gave herself a mental slap. *He must think her a complete ninny.*

Swallowing a smile, Ewan nodded. The lovely shade of pink on Daria's cheeks told of her discomfort. He'd give a pound to find out what she'd been thinking. "A break is in order, dinnae you think?"

She checked the watch on her bodice and jumped up. "I forgot to order lunch. Do you think Mr. Ilbert will be very angry?" She hurried to the coatrack and grabbed her hat.

"He probably hasn't noticed the time." Ewan climbed to his feet. "I'll help you."

"No. It wouldn't do to have the front office vacant if someone came in."

"Quite right." He gestured toward the stove. "I'll make fresh coffee and stall him if necessary."

"Thank you." She beamed, her face shining, then slipped out the door.

He stared at the vacant space for a long moment, then shuffled to the stove, its surface free of soot and pristine enough to eat from. The sink gleamed. He surveyed the room and smiled. In two short days, the office was unrecognizable. Spic and span, every surface was dust free. The books and periodicals were separated and organized, no longer a mishmash of piles. A small vase filled with flowers graced the table between the visitors' chairs. When had she done that?

Much brighter than he'd thought, she'd nearly mastered the typing machine, and more power to her. He hated the thing. Hunting and pecking for each letter, the tangle of the levers if he accidentally pressed two keys at the same time, and keeping the paper straight in the roller.

Her logic and analytical skills put his own to the test and were more developed than the previous secretary who had attended college and received formal training, yet she was not masculine. On the contrary. Her petite frame had just the right curves, and her blonde hair was the color of sunshine on a summer day. Blue eyes reminiscent of a robin's egg sparkled with wit and intelligence. Her fair skin was like the porcelain of his mother's tea set, smooth and luminescent. He'd told Miss Crenshaw that appearance was not important in his bride, but the young woman was a beauty. And she seemed oblivious to her allure, making her even more attractive.

He'd seen the stares from their male clients. More than just surprise to see a female employee, the men's gazes lingered on her more than was proper. More than a few ogled as she walked down the street. His fist clenched, then he shook his head and relaxed his fingers.

Her response to his jealousy had been clear. Besides, she gave him no cause for the emotion. She ignored the clients unless spoken to directly, then she was polite but aloof. Outside, she paid no attention to the men on the sidewalk.

Coffee made, he poured himself a cup, then leaned against the sink and sipped the fragrant liquid. He wrinkled his nose and set down the mug. He'd made it exactly as she'd shown him, but the brew was bitter. He grinned. She'd have something to say about his results. Gently teasing and poking fun at his less-than-stellar attempt.

Two days in the office, and she was already irreplaceable. Did Mr. Ilbert agree? Having a female secretary was unheard of, but she'd acclimated to the environment and tasks as if born to them. She mentioned the education she received and the books she'd devoured. Did he want her to continue working after they married? Would she marry him?

Miss Crenshaw had sent him the ideal bride, and her perfection had little to do with her abilities in the kitchen. Daria had accepted his apologies for being an oaf but still seemed wary on occasion. What could he do to prove his worth?

Chapter Eight

The nearly full moon lit the street and cast shadows as Ewan escorted Daria to the restaurant. A week had passed since her arrival, and they agreed a celebration was in order. She had settled into the job, but more importantly, shed the tension she initially wore like a cloak. She'd developed a routine of cleaning and straightening the office immediately, then plunging into the administrative tasks that kept the practice afloat such as billing and accounts receivable. Her portion of the ledger was blot-free, the numbers small and tidy. After lunch, she would assist him with cases. Best of all, Mr. Ilbert had thawed and now welcomed her with a cheery hello each morning, a behavior largely out of character.

But Daria had that effect on people. Her warmth and acceptance drew them like a bird to its nest, safe and approachable. She had a kind word for everyone, even the crotchety Mr. Faulkner who ran the livery. The man hadn't cracked a smile yet, but he no longer glowered at her when she approached. Ewan grinned. It was only a matter of time before the old codger fell prey to her charms.

He opened the door and gestured for her to proceed him. As she slipped past, the crisp scent of lavender wafted into his nose. He tamped down the desire to draw her close and take a deep breath.

"Ah, Mr. McKay. Nice to see you this evening. This must be Miss Burke." Dressed in a charcoal-colored suit with a dazzling white shirt and string tie, the gray-haired owner bowed. "It's wonderful to meet the woman who has stolen your heart. You've got the best table in the house. Secluded for privacy, but with a lovely view of the mountain."

"Uh, thank you. We've made a reservation." Ewan licked his lips. Fortunately, the man had continued to talk precluding the need for a response to his comment.

Daria beamed at the man as if he'd just handed her a puppy. "We appreciate your consideration, Mr...?"

"My apologies, miss. Shane O'Connell. Originally from County Cork." He cocked his head. "Is that a New England accent I detect?"

"I'm from Rhode Island, but how did you know?"

"I lived in Boston when I first arrived in America. Too crowded for my taste. I much prefer the wide-open spaces here in the West."

She nodded. "And the cities grow more packed by the day."

Shane motioned the far corner of the room. "I've taken enough of your time. Let's get you two seated so you can dine." He led them to a small table nestled by a window. Silvery moonlight cut a swath on the gleaming surface. Twin candles and a bouquet of wildflowers graced the center.

Ewan held Daria's chair, and her scent assailed him as she sat. Was her hair as silky as it appeared? He hurried to his seat.

"No menu tonight, Mr. McKay. We've taken the liberty of preparing a meal just for the two of you."

"To what do we owe the honor?" He eyed O'Connell. "Are you trying to gain favors with the law firm?"

Shane held up his hands in surrender. "Not at all. We wanted to welcome Miss Burke in a big way."

Daria squeezed his hand. "Don't be so suspicious, Ewan."

His skin sizzled at her touch, and his breath caught. "You're right. Sorry, O'Connell. Thanks for the effort."

"I understand, Mr. McKay. No need to apologize." He put his fingers to his forehead in a salute. "Now, just relax and enjoy your meal." He turned and wended his way through the room into the kitchen.

The moon's luminescence shone through the window, creating a halo around Daria's face. His toes curled. My, but she was a gorgeous woman. "I guess I overreacted. Dinnae mean to cast a pall over our festivities."

"You didn't. I admire your efforts to protect the firm and its reputation."

"Exactly. One can't be too careful."

"You're a man of great integrity, Ewan. I appreciate that more than you know."

He straightened. Having her admiration was the first step. Could he transform that esteem into fondness and then love?

Before he could answer, O'Connell returned with two plates of steaming food and put them on the table. "Steak, medium rare with garlic mashed potatoes and broccoli steamed to perfection. Be sure to save room for blueberry pie."

Daria clasped her hands together in front of her chin and inhaled deeply. "Perfection, indeed. This smells divine. Give our compliments to the chef."

"Will do." He bowed again, then turned on his heel and walked away.

She grinned. "Hurry and say the blessing so we can dig in."

He chuckled. "Yes, ma'am." He resisted the urge to take her hands, instead lacing his fingers in his lap. "Dear heavenly Father, thank You for the opportunity to spend time getting acquainted. Thank You for Daria's willingness to come to Wyoming and to help us in the firm. Bless our food and the folks who made it. Help us seek You in all we do. In Jesus' name, amen."

Her cheeks were slightly pink as she picked up her fork. "No one has ever thanked God for me before. Maybe my parents, but they have to, right?"

"I believe He sent you to me." He searched her face. "Don't you?"

"I've wondered, but I dared not hope. Everything came together so quickly. I mean, I prayed for help, and then Rosamund showed me Miss Crenshaw's advertisement. And she was in Newport visiting friends. How much of a coincidence is that? The next thing I knew I was chugging my way west."

"Providential not coincidental. God provides for His children." Hilda's face came to mind, and he huffed a sign. If only he'd been paying better attention, but fortunately God had been able to use the timing for both him and Daria.

"Thank you for reminding me. You're right." She scooped potatoes into her mouth and moaned. After swallowing, she said, "Who knew mashed potatoes could be so flavorful and delicious. I'll have to learn Mr. O'Connell's secret."

"A bright lass like you can figure it out. You're smarter than most of the men, myself included."

She ducked her head. "Now, you're just being polite."

"No, I'm not. It's the Irish who kiss the Blarney Stone, not the Scotch. God strike me dead if I'm lying." He winked. "I should tell you about when I first arrived in America. It's a wonder I survived."

She giggled. "That's being a fish out of water, not stupidity. Did you speak the language? Nothing was familiar, I would imagine. Kind of like me in Wyoming."

"Aye. We'll be fish together."

"I'd like that." Her face shone as if lit from within.

What had he done to deserve such a beauty?

Chapter Nine

Dappled sunlight filtered through the trees as Daria strolled toward the law firm. Despite being nearly July, the morning air held a slight chill, and she pulled her jacket closer. The sidewalk held few pedestrians, and those who walked the streets seemed intent upon their business, looking neither left nor right. Birdsong surrounded her, and she cocked her ear trying to identify the various chirps and calls.

She'd awakened early, and memories from the previous evening washed over her. Time had flown, yet every moment seemed etched in her mind. Ewan leaning toward her, his eyes changing from ice-blue to the color of the sky at dusk, depending on the topic of conversation. He laughed often, his chest rumbling with the sound. She'd been stuffed after the meal so declined dessert, but he'd insisted she have at least one bite. He'd fed her from his fork, the gesture holding an unexpected sense of intimacy.

He'd arranged for a carriage ride, complete with liveried driver. The conveyance had been open, allowing for propriety as well as magnificent views. Well-versed on the history of the town, he regaled her with story after story, bringing the town's founders to life. His singsong brogue rose and fell as she clung to his words. A perfect evening from start to finish, one she'd never expected after their initial meeting.

Her lips twisted, and she nibbled the inside of her cheek. Who was the genuine Ewan McKay? The irascible grouch or the solicitous romantic? A sigh escaped, and she increased her pace. Lollygagging would make her late, and the acceptance she'd found from Mr. Ilbert would disappear.

Two doors up, Dr. Nolan stepped out of the diner. A smile bloomed on his face, and his eyes lit up. "Good morning, Miss Burke. How are you faring?"

"Quite well. Thank you for asking." She nodded as she drew next to him. "After our...uh...rocky start, Mr. McKay and I are getting along, and I'm working at his law firm. Their secretary quit, putting them in dire straits."

"Are you enjoying the work?"

"More than I thought possible. It is both challenging and fascinating."

He cocked his head. "A female secretary. Highly irregular. Your Mr. McKay must be quite progressive."

"Actually, his boss, Mr. Ilbert, is the one who agreed to hire me, albeit temporarily. He, too, finds the idea highly irregular, as you say." She shrugged. "But in the meantime, I am feeling useful and meeting many folks. How are you settling in? Have you seen any patients yet?"

"Business is slow, but steady." He tugged at his collar. "As I'm able to help people, word will get out of my skills."

"I'll be sure to recommend you to our clients."

"That would be most appreciated." He doffed his hat. "May I see you to your office?"

Daria hesitated. Would Ewan object to the doctor keeping her company, even if only for a short distance? He'd taken an instant dislike to Dr. Nolan, but that was before he knew the man was a widower with no designs on her. After last night, Ewan must know she was committed to him. "The office is not far up the street. An escort would be lovely."

"Excellent." He clamped his bowler on his head, then clasped his hands behind his back. "I'll be sending for my children by the end of the month, and I'd love for you to meet them. My sister will be accompanying them."

"I look forward to it. I'm sure you'll be glad to have their company."

"Yes, but at the moment I'm working long hours getting the office set up and the house in tiptop shape. The previous owner didn't understand the concept of maintenance, so there is much to be done to make it livable."

"I'd be happy to help. Ewan and I both." Daria pursed her lips. "I'm quite adept at cleaning."

His forehead creased. "I wouldn't want to put you out."

"It would be no trouble—" She froze, and her jaw dropped as she stared into the café. Ewan and a dark-haired, young woman sat at a table near the window, laughing and smiling, seemingly with eyes only for each other. Well-coifed and wearing a silk dress, her hand rested on his arm.

Daria's stomach lurched, and she yanked on Dr. Nolan's sleeve. "Come. I can't be late." She hurried down the wooden sidewalk, her hands clenched at her sides. Should she confront Ewan about the woman when he arrived at work? Should she resign, take her earnings, and flee town? No, two weeks' wages was not enough for a new start. She'd have to save for much longer. Who was the woman? Ewan claimed to have no marital prospects. Yet he seemed rather cozy with the woman. Was he lying about having no relationships? He was a believer. How could he treat her this way?

They arrived at the law firm, and she yanked open the door. "Thank you for the escort, doctor, but I have a busy day ahead of me."

"Are you all right?"

"Fine. I'll see you again soon." She marched inside and let the door close behind her. She owed the poor man an explanation, but now wasn't the time. She straightened her spine. Nor was it the time to make a decision about Ewan, but one thing was certain: she would tamp down her growing attraction for the man since nothing could obviously come from the relationship.

Squinting into the morning sun, Ewan rushed down the sidewalk to the office. The client meeting had gone longer than anticipated, but it was finally over and he would see Daria. He'd have preferred that Mr. Ilbert meet with the heiress, Clara Quaite, but he'd begged off claiming too much work. In reality, his boss probably didn't want to be subjected to the woman's predatory manner.

A shudder slithered up Ewan's spine. She'd clung to him like a leech when he helped her out of the carriage, then repeatedly touched his hands and arm through the course of their meal. He'd had to remind her to keep her voice down on numerous occasions. Why she thought discussing her personal situation in public was beyond him. The rich in America were different from the gentry in Europe.

The town came alive as he walked. Merchants opened their shops, and foot traffic got heavier. Hordes of men interspersed with the occasional woman or family. Wagons rattled down the street, mingling with the *clip-clop* of horses' hooves. Shouts combined with the hum of conversations. Nothing like Scotland, Rocky Mountain Springs had grown on him, and he might not feel like an American yet, but the small town was home. Hopefully, Daria would come to the same conclusion sooner rather than later.

Daria. A vision of her face floated into his mind, and he stepped up his pace.

In front of the law office, he stopped and smoothed his suit jacket and pants, then inspected his reflection in the window. As good as it would get. He opened the door and smiled. Back to him, Daria was busy dusting the bookshelves, her skirts swaying in a tantalizing manner as she made her way down the room. He cleared his throat. "Good morning."

She whirled, and her eyes narrowed. "Good morning." Her tone was stilted, and she returned to her task.

His eyebrow lifted. Where was the warm welcome he expected after their delightful evening? What had happened between then and now? Or was her mood more evidence of a volatile nature? How deeply had Miss Crenshaw investigated his bride-to-be?

Ewan hung his bowler on the rack, then shed his jacket, placing it on the hook. He rolled up his sleeves and strode to his desk. Behind on his tasks because of the clingy Miss Quaite, he'd leave Daria be for the moment. First, he'd write the report about the heiress, indicating his recommendation about taking the woman's case, or not, as was his preference. He wanted nothing more to do with her, but business was business. If the firm based their caseload on whether or not they got along with a potential client, they'd have few lawsuits to handle.

He seated himself and dove into his tasks. Finished with the summary of his meeting, he waved the document, then laid it aside. "Miss Burke, would you please take this to Mr. Ilbert?"

Her chin lifted, and her lips thinned. "You are too busy to deliver it yourself?"

"As a matter of fact, I am." His eyes widened. "I'm late getting started and have much to accomplish today."

She mumbled something he couldn't hear, then snatched up the paper and stalked into Mr. Ilbert's office.

Was she angry at his tardiness? Had she expected him to fawn over her after last night? She must know that would be inappropriate in the office. If they wed, would she be a temperamental shrew for the remainder of their lives? Did he want to marry her? Perhaps it wasn't too late to pay her way back to Rhode Island. Or anywhere else she wished to go.

Chapter Ten

Miss Quaite entered the law office in a swish of silk and cloud of flowery perfume. Daria's face warmed as she exchanged a look with Ewan. He'd pressed her into telling him why she was upset, and she'd accused him of a relationship with the woman in the diner. He'd gaped at her, then his face had darkened and taken on distant stare. He assured her there was nothing improper between them, although he understood why she might believe that. After a lengthy conversation, they put the misunderstanding behind them, but now the woman was here.

Dressed in an emerald-green dress with copious ruffles, the heiress was the picture of wealth. Her matching hat was a confection of ribbons and lace, perched at a jaunty angle atop her flaxen ringlets. Piercing blue eyes met Daria's, reminding her of a hawk she'd seen as a child. She shuddered but pinned on a smile. She had a feeling her stepmother was a novice manipulator compared to this woman.

"Who have we here?" Miss Quaite glided toward her, arching one perfectly shaped eyebrow. "I'd heard you had a female secretary, Mr. McKay. How progressive of you."

Daria resisted the urge to pat her hair or check her hands for ink. Instead, she dipped her head in acknowledgment. "I'm Daria Burke. It's a pleasure to meet you, Miss Quaite."

"You know my name?"

"I'm versed on all our cases."

The woman waved her fan. "Of course you are. You must be very clever." Her tone indicated she didn't believe her own words.

"Would you like some coffee or tea, Miss Quaite?"

"No, thank you." She dug into her pocketbook, leather with a green velvet flap, and pulled out a sheaf of papers that she handed to Ewan. "This is the information you requested." Her eyes raked him from head to toe. "I'd be happy to set up an appointment to review them with you." She stroked his arm, then winked.

Swallowing a gasp, Daria stuffed her clenched fists into her pockets. She would not let the vixen see her shock. Or let the tentacles of jealousy entrap her.

"Thank you, Miss Quaite." Ewan opened the door. "I'll let you know if further discussion is required. Mr. Ilbert and I appreciate you delivering this personally."

The heiress tapped his chest with her fan. "I look forward to hearing from you." She sent a glance over her shoulder at Daria, then sashayed out of the office.

Ewan heaved out a huge breath and rolled his eyes as he closed the door. "Well, that was...awkward."

With a sigh, Daria moved to her chair and sat down. "You were the perfect gentleman. Do you need me to do anything with the information she brought or will you take it directly to Mr. Ilbert?"

"I'll review it first, then give it to him with my recommendations." He finger-combed his hair, tossed the pages onto his desk, then went to the stove and poured two cups of coffee. "I have a feeling we're going to need this."

The door swung open, and Sheriff Jeffries filled the entrance with his huge frame. He removed his hat, and a shock of black hair fell over his forehead, shadowing his dark eyes. He surveyed the room, his gaze falling on Daria.

Her pulse skittered. Something told her life was about to change for the worse. Just when she'd thought her painful past was behind her.

He held up a folded document, an expression of chagrin on his face. "This is a warrant to search your hotel room for stolen goods, Miss Burke."

"What?" Ewan slammed the mugs on the counter and rushed forward to stand behind her. "You cannae possibly be serious."

Her vision swam, and she fought to keep down her breakfast. She clutched the edge of her desk with cold fingers.

"I'm afraid I am, Ewan. The warrant explains everything," he said as he extended his hand with the paper.

Ewan snatched the warrant and scanned the sheet, then snorted. "Surely you realize this isn't possible. Miss Burke isn't a thief."

Tears filled her eyes, and her chin trembled. There was only one person who could have made this happen. Amaryllis had somehow found her and was out for revenge. Or to simply ensure Daria's misery. She wrapped her hand around her locket, her only connection to her parents.

"How did she find me?" Daria's voice was a ragged whisper.

He laid his hand on her shoulder, the warmth of his fingers sending a tingle down her back. "If she was smart, she used a Pinkerton detective. Those folks are among the best in the nation."

Her chin trembled. "But I didn't steal anything of hers."

"This warrant says differently. There is a list of specific items."

Daria shook off Ewan's hand, swiped the moisture from her face, and climbed to her feet. She pulled herself to her full height and met the sheriff's eyes. "You are welcome to search my room, Sheriff Jeffries. I did not take anything from my stepmother, and I have nothing to hide." She raised tear-filled eyes to him. "If there's no proof, can he arrest me?"

"The burden of proof occurs during the trial. And if he doesnae find the items indicated on the warrant, he cannae arrest you or take you into custody." Ewan glared at the sheriff. "Can you give me a moment with my client, Jeffries?"

"Uh, sure. I'll be right outside."

"I'm sure you will." Cupping her elbow, he led her to the upholstered chairs.

She sank into the cushions. Tears threatened again, but she blinked them away. She would not fall apart. She couldn't.

"First, I want you to know I believe you're innocent, so start from the beginning, and tell me why your stepmother would hunt you down with false claims." He laced his fingers with her and drew gentle circles on the back of her hand. "I cannae help you unless I know absolutely everything."

Heart pounding, Daria frowned. "I see what we charge clients, and I can't afford to pay you."

He grinned. "We'll take it out of your pay."

Her eyes widened. "But—"

"I'm sorry. That was bad form." His faced reddened. "I thought a bit of levity would cheer you. The firm will represent you at no cost."

A shaky laugh escaped, and she searched his face. His expression held no judgment, only contrition and concern. The tension slipped from her muscles. She would trust him. With a nod, she licked her lips and recounted all that had happened since she was a child. Her mother's death and her father's grief. The time period when it was just the two of them, then how life changed when he married Amaryllis. And the nightmare that began after her father died. The culmination of events on the fateful day she'd seen her stepmother and stepsisters prancing out of the house wearing her mother's clothes and jewelry. "They're the thieves, not me."

"Then we will get to the bottom of their charges." He squeezed her fingers. "As well as what went on after your father died. It appears there is more here than meets the eye, and we will find it."

Daria slumped against the back of the chair. Perhaps there was reason for a shred of hope.

Chapter Eleven

Her gaze riveted on the wooden sidewalk, Daria clung to Ewan's arm as she trudged toward the hotel, the sheriff on her heels. Her knees quivered and threatened to buckle. Her stomach fluttered as if a flock of hummingbirds had taken flight. Did she dare to raise her head to see the stares and censure of the townspeople? A cluster of men stood in the street outside the saloon, and their conversation died as she approached.

Ewan tipped his hat as if they were on a Sunday stroll. "Gentlemen." He leaned toward her. "If you look guilty, people will assume you are. Meet their eyes and smile."

She lifted her chin and straightened her spine. Forcing her lips into a smile, she nodded to the men. Ewan was right. She'd almost let Amaryllis and her daughter crush her spirit. She'd wouldn't let strangers do the same thing. Lengthening her stride, she marched to the door of the lodging establishment and led the men inside.

The lobby was vacant except for the desk clerk and a pair of elegantly dressed men chatting near the fireplace. Both wore pin-striped suits of charcoal gray. Their shoes gleamed, and their hair was slicked with pomade.

"Well done, lass."

Warmth filled her at the admiration in his eyes. *Thank You, God, for this man. I don't know what the future holds, especially with Amaryllis's machinations, but help me rest in Your plans. Help me to point others to You during this difficult time.*

Her smile broadened as peace settled on her shoulders like a cloak in wintertime. "My room is upstairs, Sheriff Jeffries." After a nod to the clerk, she gestured toward the stairs. "Ewan, I can take care of this if you'd like to wait here."

"Oh, no. I'll be with you the entire time." He laced his fingers with hers. "As your fiancé *and* your attorney. Two are better than one, but three are best," he whispered. "I've been praying since the sheriff waved that warrant at us. It may not feel like it, but God is in control."

She squeezed his hand. "Thank you."

Their shoes scraped on the steps, then they were in the upstairs corridor. Daria's heart pounded, and she took a deep breath before digging her key from her reticule. Her hand shook, and the knob rattled in her palm as she swung open the door. The room seemed to shrink with the men's presence.

Looking at it through their eyes, she cringed at her weathered trunk and plain toiletries. The sheriff opened the armoire, revealing her worn clothing. She'd meant to speak to Ewan about her attire, but there never seemed to be enough time. Besides, she would not stoop to asking him for money to refurbish her wardrobe. She'd planned to do that with the money she earned at the law firm.

Sheriff Jeffries sent her an apologetic glance, then began to rifle through her garments one by one, running his fingers into the pockets and along the hems. Finding nothing, he moved to the dresser and opened the drawers. Her face scorched as his calloused hands picked up her undergarments, and Ewan had the grace to study the floor as if it were the most interesting thing he'd ever seen. Fortunately, she had few items, so the search took mere seconds.

He looked inside the pitcher on top of the dresser, then jerked his head toward the trunk. "That thing locked?"

"No, Sheriff. There's nothing inside."

With a flick of his wrist, he opened the chest and peered into the empty box. He dropped the lid with a crash.

"Have a care, Jeffries." Ewan frowned.

"Sorry." The lawman had the grace to look abashed, then crouched to peek under the bed. He rose, scanning the small space. His shoulders slumped, and his gaze rested on her face.

"Disappointed at not finding whatever it is my stepmother claims I stole?" Daria unsuccessfully kept the triumph from her voice. "I told you I didn't take anything."

"Maybe you're clever enough not to stash the goods here."

Her stomach tightened. Would she go to jail because of false claims?

Ewan held up his hands. "Look, you've done what you came to do without success. I suggest you leave."

"Fair enough, but this isn't over, Miss Burke."

"I understand, Sheriff."

Her chin trembled, and she pressed her lips together. So much for a fresh start, but perhaps with Ewan's help she had hope.

Daria's shoulders sagged, and Ewan squelched the desire to draw her into his arms and stroke her head. Their relationship was nowhere near that sort of intimacy. He'd speak to Jeffries later about treating her as a common criminal. The man had been doing his job, but did he have to act as if he believed the charges? "We'll head back to the firm and meet with Mr. Ilbert. He'll know what to do." He sent her an encouraging smile. "He's also very well connected. He won't do anything untoward, but he'll have access to information we don't."

She huffed out a sigh, and his heart constricted. She looked like she'd lost her best friend.

He gestured to the door. "We should probably head out."

Her face pinked. "True. No reason to feed the rumor mill."

"Exactly." He led her downstairs and out the door, his hand on the small of her back. Once outside, he offered her his arm, and she slipped her hand in the crook of his elbow. They walked toward the law office. "I haven't had a chance to tell you, but I know how you feel. My father was wronged unjustly, and our family lost everything as a result. I was clerking for a barrister, but he sacked me when word got out about Da. He didn't want an employee who was stained. It would look bad for his practice. No one else would hire me, so I decided to try my hand in America. Maybe I'll learn enough over here to help me prove his innocence."

"Oh, Ewan, how awful." Her lips turned down, and her forehead creased. "He's—?"

"A guest of Her Majesty, Queen Victoria."

"I'm so sorry. Does Mr. Ilbert know?"

"Yes, I told him everything during the interview. He doesn't believe the sins of the father should be visited on the son."

"But your father isn't guilty."

"In the eyes of society he is." He shrugged. "Fortunately, Mr. Ilbert has a friend in England who has taken Da's case, so I pray and wait."

"And I will pray with you."

Ewan's chest swelled. Entangled in her own legal problems, yet Daria committed to intercede for his father. A special lass, to be sure. "But enough about me." He opened the door to the firm, and they froze.

Mr. Ilbert stood on the threshold of his office. "I've been waiting for you. Jeffries stopped by here after he searched the hotel room."

"I'm sorry for the uproar, Mr. Ilbert. I hope you believe I'm innocent."

"Of course you are, my girl." He cocked his head. "Don't you think I conducted a background check? You're clean as a whistle. Now, that stepmother of yours is another story." He rubbed his hands together. "But as Mr. McKay knows, it will be a matter of convincing the courts, so we have our work cut out for us. Best get to it."

Ewan's breath whooshed out of him. He'd promised Daria his boss would take her case, but after the words left his mouth he'd second-guessed himself. He shouldn't have worried, yet even after telling her God was in control, he'd fretted about the situation. When would he learn?

They went into the office, and Ewan stole a glance at Daria. A tentative smile clung to her lips, and the tension had left her body. She glided across the room, her skirts swishing with her movement. Oh, to have been the one to bring that expression to her face rather than Mr. Ilbert. Hopefully he would in the not-too-distant future.

Chapter Twelve

The wooden pew bit into Daria's legs. She shifted on the seat and swallowed a sigh. Pastor Van Buren was a good speaker, his words a balm to her weary soul, but she was struggling to focus. Her problems loomed like a midwestern thunderstorm, dark and foreboding.

The sheriff continued to act as if he knew she was hiding her crime...that he'd find the stolen items in a matter of time. Word had leaked out about her, and she was now subjected to stares and speculation. Going to the mercantile usually included at least one halted conversation upon her arrival.

Mr. Ilbert assured her that he and Ewan would be able to rebut the charges. She wanted to believe him, but knowing the court system had failed Ewan's father, she was skeptical. Innocent people did go to jail. Would she be one of them?

She scanned the small congregation, and her gaze fell on two of the girls from the boarding house. When she realized the wedding Ewan wasn't in the near future, she'd suggested that she move out of the hotel to save him money. He agreed, seeming guilty, embarrassed, and relieved. The poor man continued to feel bad about his impoverished state no matter how often she assured him that wealth was of no interest to her.

Pastor Van Buren's voice pushed his way through her musings. "Beloved, it's hard to feel like God has your best interests at heart when life is difficult. If you're anything like me, you make your plans, then notify your heavenly Father so he can tag along."

Daria grimaced as a chuckle rippled through the congregation. His words rang too close to the truth. She'd tried to leave her problems with the Lord, but it seemed since no progress was being made, so she took matters into her own hands.

"In the book of Jeremiah, God reminds the prophet of His plans: plans to prosper His children, plans to provide hope and a future." The pastor smiled. "Sometimes we disagree with God's plans, don't we?"

Crossing her ankles, Daria nibbled on her lower lip. Disagree was right. Why had the Lord's plans included her parents dying and being mistreated by Amaryllis and her daughters? Why had He allowed them to get away with deceitful behaviors, inheriting what was rightfully hers? And now, subject her to false charges that might result in her going to prison.

Stomach tight, she forced her attention on the preacher.

The pastor paused and held up his Bible, an expectant silence filling the church. Even the little ones were quiet.

A breeze wafted through the windows and stroked her face. *Is that You, God? Are You really there? Are You the Grand Chess Master, moving us like pawns on a board, or did You set the world to spinning and walk away? Do you manage humanity or leave us to our own devices?*

She wasn't sure how she felt about either answer.

Beside her, Ewan glanced over, concern lining his face.

Her cheeks heated. She'd been caught fidgeting like a child. She sent him what she hoped was a reassuring smile, then turned her gaze to the preacher who continued to exhort and encourage the crowd. Had the man ever had a difficult day in his life? Did he know of what he spoke? It was easy to claim God is in control when things are working well and blessings abound. What about when adversity attacked from every corner?

"Our life here on earth is beset by challenges. In several of the Psalms, King David complains about evildoers not getting caught, in fact, succeeding in their nefarious deeds. It's not fair, when those who seek to do wrong do better than those of us who try to walk the straight and narrow. In the book of Matthew, Jesus indicates that the rain falls on the just and the unjust. Kind of feels like He's pouring salt in the wound by saying that." Pastor Van Buren beamed at the crowd, his gaze moving from one person to another, until his eyes landed on her as he said, "But He's not being mean. That verse is often taken out of context. This section of His sermon is telling us how to behave as His followers. We're to love our enemies, even pray for them. A hard command, to be sure."

Daria fought the urge to flee. God wanted her to love Amaryllis? Pansy and Magnolia, too? And worse, for her to pray for them. He asked too much.

"God asks too much of us, doesn't He?"

Her eyes widened. Was the man a mind reader?

"I've walked where you've walked, people. Been filled with hate at those who persecuted me, but love is more than an emotion. It is a choice. Forgiveness is a choice. Following our Lord is a choice. One we have to make each and every day. One that isn't easy, but is worth the resulting peace. Let us pray."

Mind racing, she squeezed her eyes closed. Pastor Van Buren had trod heavily on her toes today. Given her food for thought that she'd rather not consume.

He intoned the benediction, and the congregation rose. Conversation buzzed like a swarm of honeybees. Laughter tinkled, and footsteps clomped as people moved toward the doors.

She gathered her worn Bible to her chest, then picked up her reticule. She turned to the aisle, and her jaw dropped. Across the room, Miss Quaite stood surrounded by several of the older women. The heiress had not struck her as someone who would frequent a church. Why was she here? Was she trying to ingratiate herself to the town by attending services, or had she begun to see the error of her flirting ways? Who was Daria to judge?

The woman lifted her head, and her eyes seemed to search the room. A wide grin bloomed on her face, and she sent someone behind Daria an imperceptible nod. Turning, Daria grimaced. Gaze set on the heiress, Ewan touched his forehead in acknowledgment.

Nausea rolled over her in waves. Apparently, there was more to his relationship with Miss Quaite than he'd led Daria and Mr. Ilbert to believe. Why else would he be signaling to the woman?

"Are you ready to go, Daria?" Ewan crooked his arm.

"Uh, yes, but I must beg off for lunch. I've developed a headache." A lie that would no doubt prove to true once she returned to her room and had time to consider this latest turn of events.

Chapter Thirteen

Ewan stole a peek at Daria as they meandered down the sidewalk toward the boarding house. Dark shadows hung below her eyes in her wan face. Her lips were turned down. Even her hair looked dull and lifeless. She'd been chipper and eager to go to services when he'd arrived to escort her to church. But as the sermon progressed, she'd shifted and squirmed. Was that when she began to feel ill? Was the sudden onset of her headache a symptom of a serious sickness? "Daria, should we find the doctor?"

She glanced at him, her eyes the color of flint. "No, I'll be fine after I've had a chance to rest."

His stomach hollowed. His knowledge of women was minimal, but she seemed more upset than ill, and she hadn't exhibited a delicate constitution since her arrival. Had the pastor said something that pricked her heart? Had the sermon uncovered bad memories?

Maybe she was simply overwhelmed from the events of the last couple of days. He certainly wouldn't be at his best with charges of theft hanging over his head. She fit in so well, it was hard to remember she'd only been in Rocky Mountain Springs three weeks.

The changes and upheaval she'd experienced would rattle the strongest of men. He patted her hand. "We'll get through this. It's terrible right now with all the uncertainty associated with the case, but Mr. Ilbert is the smartest man I've ever known. He'll help us get to the bottom of your situation."

"I appreciate the efforts the two of you are making for me." Her voice wavered. "This is one of the few times since Father died that I've been taken seriously. Miss Crenshaw did, and now you. Your support means a lot."

"It saddens me to know you were so oppressed." He swallowed past the lump in his throat. What sort of person persecutes a young girl? "Was there no one within the house who treated you well?"

"Rosamunde." Her mouth quirked. "She was one of the maids and had been with the family from the beginning. She was with my mother before that. Amaryllis didn't scare her. In fact, sometimes it seemed that Rosamunde went out of her way to agitate her. She quit when I left. Said she'd only plan to stay until I was gone."

"She's the one who told you about Miss Crenshaw?"

"Yes." She sighed. "I miss her."

"Then we shall find her, so you can have a reunion. Would you like that?"

Her eyes lit. "Very much."

He snapped his fingers. "In fact, we should begin looking for her immediately. She would make an excellent witness to what went on in your father's house. First thing tomorrow, I'll send a telegram to the Denver office of the Pinkerton Agency." He straightened his spine. "It shouldnae take them long to find her. She could also tell us if there were other staff who might give us insight. This may break the case wide open." He grinned at Daria, but his smile faltered at her lack of excitement. "I'm sorry. I'm blathering on, and you're feeling poorly. We're almost to the boarding house."

"Most of the servants feared Amaryllis. I doubt they will tell you what you want to know. She would rain down unimaginable retribution."

"Was she never loving to you?"

"She and my father were besotted with each other, and in the beginning she ignored me. But she became jealous of the time he and I spent together, so she would try to cause disagreements between us. When that didn't work, she devised reasons for us to be separated. It wasn't until after he died that she became verbally abusive and relegated me to servant status."

His pulse quickened. "Was she ever...physical?"

"The occasional slap until I grew old enough to fight back." Daria rubbed her cheek, then lifted her shoulder in a half-hearted shrug. "In many ways, I was happier among the staff. They had their problems, but they were genuine. None of the lying and subterfuge that went on upstairs. The deviousness. Her so-called friends were just as bad. Posturing and putting on affectations as if they were royalty." She frowned and slanted a glance at him. "I hate the artifice and the intentional misleading that some people do."

"Aye."

They arrived at the boarding house. "If you continue to feel under the weather tomorrow, don't come into the office. I'll explain to Mr. Ilbert."

"I'll be there." She narrowed her eyes. "I'm a woman of my word."

"Yes, but we don't expect you to work when you're ill."

"Unlike others, I keep *my* commitments. Thank you for walking me home. I'll see you in the morning." She stepped inside and closed the door.

He stuffed his hands into his pockets and stared at the house. What had just happened? In the span of a morning, her moods had swung from lively to unrest to scorn and finally seemingly to anger. At him. Dinnae she want his help? She'd seemed to until today.

She was a beautiful woman, bright and witty, but then the dragon appeared out of nowhere. Who was this lass? What was the real reason for her erratic behavior?

Chapter Fourteen

Daria pressed a hand to her stomach and licked her dry lips as she hesitated in front of the door to the law firm. She'd wrestled with her feelings throughout yesterday afternoon, her head throbbing as anticipated. Then her gaze had fallen on her father's Bible gathering dust on the nightstand. Tears brimming, she sat in the rocker cradling the supple leather volume to her chest for a long while. Then she'd flipped through the tissue-paper pages, reading snippets of passages and Father's spidery handwriting along the margins. Finally, she decided she'd imagined the interaction between Ewan and Miss Quaite, and peace had descended. She crawled into bed and slept soundly until the sun peeked through the gauzy curtains of her room.

She owed Ewan an apology for her snippy behavior. Her cheeks warmed, and she took a deep breath. Standing outside the office would only delay the inevitable. Hopefully, he would be gracious enough to forgive her. She shuddered. With her waffling conduct, he might put her on the next train back to Rhode Island.

With a tight grip on the knob, she entered the office. Ewan looked up, his face expressionless. He obviously wondered which of her personalities she brought today. She hurried to her desk, knees trembling. "Thank you again for escorting me home yesterday. I-I'm feeling better, and...uh...I'm sorry for how I acted. You must think me a shrew." She dropped into her chair. "I'll try not to be so prickly in the future."

"To be honest, I was concerned and a bit taken aback." A smile bloomed on his face. "But today is a new day. Let's move forward. I've sent the telegram to the Pinkerton Agency, but it may be a couple of days before we receive a reply. If it's not too burdensome, could you create a list of the other servants and where you think their loyalties lie?"

"A good idea." Her pulse tripped. He didn't fault her for yesterday. What a compassionate and considerate man. "Then if we find Rosamunde we can see if she agrees with my assessment." She glanced at the stove where the coffee was already warming. "You made the coffee. Did you think I wouldn't come?"

"I wasnae sure, but I wanted you to be able to have some right away if you did." He sent her a wry grin. "Although, we know mine is not nearly as delicious as yours."

With a giggle, she rose, and the pressure in her chest eased. "It's the thought that counts." She tucked her reticule in the drawer and pulled out a dust cloth. "No lollygagging yet. I'll clean, then take a break."

He winked. "Suit yourself."

Daria's breath caught. Why had God blessed her with such a devastatingly handsome and spirit-filled man? She didn't deserve His favor. She made quick work of her chores, sneaking peeks at Ewan as she dusted, swept, and straightened the office. She delivered Mr. Ilbert's coffee at the appointed hour, then settled at her desk to draft the list of household staff.

Tapping the pencil on her chin, she forced herself to revisit her childhood home. Memories assailed her, some sweet, some painful, others a combination of the two. She pushed aside the bad recollections and focused on the good. To a person, the servants had been supportive and respectful, drawing alongside her in gracious companionship. How had she missed that? She'd taken their friendship for granted, at some level being no better than Amaryllis.

"Are you okay?" Ewan's voice broke through her reverie. "Your face tells me your trip down Memory Lane has resurrected many emotions."

"More than I expected." She frowned. "The worst part is that I realize I never told the staff how much they meant to me. They must think me totally ungrateful."

"I'm sure they know, but you may see them in connection with the case." He rose and slid into his jacket, a lock of dark brown hair falling over his tanned forehead. "I've got business to attend to and will be out for the rest of the day. I'm sorry we won't be able to do lunch, but I'll pick you up for dinner at six o'clock. How does that sound?"

"Perfect." She fiddled with the paper. "Is there anything I can do to assist you with your business?"

He nodded. "Aye. Please go to the courthouse some time after three o'clock and pick up a package for me. I'll let them know you'll be the one coming for the deeds." He wagged his finger at her. "Now, don't work too hard."

She put her fingers to her head in a mock salute. "Aye-aye, sir."

Chuckling, he picked up his leather satchel and strode out of the office, leaving the room feeling empty. He was not a gregarious man, but his presence filled the space. She sighed and went back to her task, then after a quick lunch, she copied reports, created files, and typed documents until her fingers cramped.

The clock struck three, and she stretched, her spine snapping with the movement. She retrieved her reticule and climbed to her feet. She went to Mr. Ilbert's door and knocked on the frame. "Mr. McKay asked me to pick up some files from the courthouse. Is now a convenient time for me to do that, sir?"

He gave her a distracted wave. "Fine. Fine. I'd rather not be disturbed, so please lock up."

"Will do." She secured the office and strolled toward the courthouse. An odiferous breeze filled with the smell of dirt, manure, and animals filled the air and tugged at her skirts, making her wish for the crispy, briny air of Newport. She glanced at the shop displays, then caught sight of Ewan's reflection in the glass of one of the stores. She turned with a smile, then gasped. He and Miss Quaite chatted and laughed as they headed into the hotel. *The hotel?*

Daria's stomach clenched, and she closed her eyes. No. No. No. This couldn't be happening. She'd convinced herself last night that nothing perverse was going on between the two, but was she wrong? Was Ewan playing her for a fool? Stringing her along while pursuing a relationship with the heiress? He claimed he didn't miss the money his father had lost, but someone of his stature was used to wealth. Scraping by on a law clerk's salary had to be frustrating. The woman was obviously smitten with him. She'd made that clear during her visit to the firm.

What to do? March across the street and confront them? Pretend she hadn't seen them? Ewan couldn't possibly be an answer to her prayers for a husband. But would God allow her to develop feelings if her intended wasn't the faith-filled believer he claimed to be?

There had to be an innocent explanation, but what was it? She gritted her teeth, marched to the courthouse, and picked up the documents. Head down, she returned to the office and closed the door with a bang.

Standing next to the stove, a cup of coffee in his hand, Mr. Ilbert started. "Why all the ruckus, Miss Burke? You look madder than an old wet hen."

"I'm sorry, sir." Her cheeks warmed, and she blurted, "I won't go into details, but your employee may not be the stand-up guy you think."

The lawyer set down his cup. "Keep in mind that not all things are as they appear, my dear."

"Exactly." She dropped into her chair. "A fine birthday this turned out to be."

Chapter Fifteen

"Daria?" A knocked sounded, and Sally, one of her housemates, spoke through the door. "Mr. McKay is here for you."

"Thank you."

"Don't be too long. He's a looker." Sally giggled. "Ada or Bridget might snatch him up."

"I'll be right down." Daria frowned at her reflection. She pinched her cheeks to give them some color, then grabbed her shawl. No matter how warm the days were, the nights carried a chill. She picked up her reticule, then left the room, locking the door behind her. Before she accompanied Ewan to the restaurant, she would have it out with him about the heiress. She squared her shoulders and descended the stairs.

Standing in the foyer with his Stetson in hand, Ewan looked every inch the rich man he used to be. His brown hair was slicked back and curled slightly at his collar. Crystal-blue eyes twinkled as he smiled, his teeth white against his tanned face. His gray suit fit him as if hand-tailored, his boots buffed to a high shine. "You look lovely, lass. Are you ready to go?"

Her heart pounded, and she licked her lips, suddenly gone dry. My, but wasn't he attractive. She took a deep breath and shook her head. "Not yet. There's something I wish to discuss with you."

His eyebrows came together. "Sounds serious."

"It may be. Let's go into the parlor for privacy."

He nodded, his expression wary, and followed her into the small room abutting the entryway. He gestured to the overstuffed sofa in front of the fireplace. "Would you like to sit down?"

"Yes. No." She wrapped her arms around her middle. "No, this won't take long." And she dare not sit close to him. His familiar scent of leather, bay rum, and essence unique to him would distract her, sending her thoughts out the window. "I need you to tell me once and for all that nothing is going on between you and Miss Quaite."

"What?" His eyes widened, and confusion clouded his eyes. "Why would you think that? I already told you I have no interest in her."

"Then why did I see the two of you entering the hotel this afternoon? You seemed quite cozy."

Ewan blew out a loud breath, then motioned to the couch. "Come, let's sit down."

She hesitated, her glance bouncing from his face to the sofa.

"Please." His voice caressed her. "This is much too serious to discuss standing in the center of the room."

With a nod, she marched over and dropped onto the cushion.

He lowered himself beside her and placed his hat on his knee. With a gentle finger, he raised her chin until she met his eyes, then dropped his hand. "There is no romantic relationship between me and Miss Quaite. She is a friend and a client, nothing more. She is the American cousin of a family I knew back in Scotland, from the same social circles. Her relatives were the only ones who didn't abandon us after the incident with my father."

"She seems to desire more."

"That's her way." His lips twisted. "She's flirty, and I've told her those actions will get her into trouble one day, but she persists."

Daria narrowed her eyes and studied his face. There seemed to be no guile in his expression, but many a member of the gentry had mastered the look of innocence. "I don't know..."

Ewan laced his fingers with hers. "I understand your lack of trust. You've suffered greatly from people who say one thing yet do another. We will get together with Clara, and you will hear directly from her that we are just friends. Will that help?"

She shrugged. "I suppose so."

"Tell you what, I will not see Clara alone. If we meet about her case, we'll do so in the office. And there will be no socializing. Period."

"I'm being silly, aren't I?"

He squeezed her hand. "Not at all. You've been hurt. Badly. Now, I'd like to take you to dinner at the hotel. Their chef is excellent, and we'll order the best they have. We can start fresh with a clean slate. Will you go with me?"

"Yes." She extricated her hand and rose. "Thank you for understanding. For not brushing aside my fears."

"Never." He stood, picked up her shawl, and wrapped it around her shoulders. "The restaurant isnae far, but I've borrowed Mr. Ilbert's carriage and driver. We will arrive in style."

She slipped her hand through the crook, his warmth sending tingles from her fingers to the top of her head. She gulped. Had he felt her tremble?

They left the house, and he helped her into the carriage. The door closed, and the setting sun cast shadows on the seats. His aroma filled the enclosure, and moisture sprang to her palms. How could he affect her so strongly? Only three weeks had elapsed since she'd set foot in Wyoming.

Moments later, they stopped in front of the restaurant, and the door swung open, the driver standing at attention. He assisted her to the ground, then Ewan stepped out behind her. He led her up the stairs, his hand on the small of her back. Heat seared her skin at his touch. They went inside, and she froze. The room was vacant and shrouded in darkness. "What?"

"Surprise! Happy birthday!" People burst through the swinging doors from the kitchen, Miss Quaite leading the charge. She hurried toward Daria and enveloped her in a fragrant hug, the woman's perfume heady and strong.

Tears sprang to Daria's eyes, and she looked at Ewan. "You threw me a surprise party? How did you know?" She turned to Miss Quaite. "And you helped?"

The woman giggled. "Helped? I ran the show." She slapped Ewan with her ever-present fan. "This one was useless."

Ewan flushed. "I wasnae totally useless."

"This is what you were doing when I saw you?" It was Daria's turn to blush. Her cheeks scorched. "I thought—"

"I'm sure you thought the worst, honey." Miss Quaite beamed at her. "I'm a terrible flirt, even with Ewan. I enjoy watching him squirm, but you can have him. He's like a brother. And now you'll be like a sister. You should call me Clara. No more of this Miss Quaite nonsense."

"You're not—"

"No, ma'am." Clara snorted a laugh. "He's all yours."

Daria gaped at Ewan.

He grinned like a cat that had finished a full bowl of cream. "Miss Crenshaw told me your birthdate. We agreed it would be fun to do something since you'd still be new to town." His smile faltered. "I feel badly that our subterfuge caused you to worry. It never occurred to me you'd see us."

Clara jabbed him with her elbow and snorted a laugh. "Small town, Ewan. You can't get away with anything. Now, enough jawing. Let's seat the guest of honor. She must be starving." She wiggled her eyebrows at Daria. "Would you like your cake first?"

"No." Daria swallowed. Her mind raced, yet she couldn't articulate more than a single word. These people hardly knew her, yet they came to celebrate her special day. Once again, she'd let her painful experiences color her thoughts and attitudes, assuming the worst about Ewan. When would she be free of her past?

Conversation buzzed around her as she followed Ewan to a table by the window set with an ivory-colored cloth and topped with gleaming china and silverware. An enormous bouquet of flowers filled a vase in the center. He held her chair as she sat down, then squeezed her shoulder before taking his own chair. The waitress delivered two steaming plates of food, then disappeared into the crowd. Thumps and bumps filled the air as the guests seated themselves.

Eyes sparkling, Ewan leaned toward her and whispered, "Happy birthday, Daria. I hope this year gives you everything you wish for."

Pulse skittering, she sighed. "I already have it."

"Not quite, but perhaps soon. I've unearthed the information we needed about your father's estate. We'll need to travel to Rhode Island to transact our business, but...uh...we shouldn't travel together as single people. Would you be willing to marry before we leave?" His face reddened. "I won't expect any sort of...uh...physical relationship until you're ready."

Her heart leapt inside her chest, and she gasped. Her toes curled. Marrying him was why she'd come to Wyoming, but now the moment was here. She could do this. She would do this. "I'd be honored to marry you."

Chapter Sixteen

The door to the church opened, and Daria appeared at the back of the church. Ewan's pulse raced. Adorned in a yellow gown, offset with a lace collar and cuffs, she seemed to glide up the aisle. Her blue eyes sparkled, and her hair was a tumble of riotous curls. A bouquet of wildflowers was in her hands. It had been a week since the surprise party when they announced their intention to marry. Rayne had sprung into action, and with an army of women, arranged decorations, music, and food for the wedding.

His bride drew alongside him, then handed the flowers to Rayne, who'd offered to stand up with her. Daria's smile was tentative, and she nibbled on her lower lip as she tended to do when she was nervous.

He could relate. Crossing the ocean to America had been less frightening. His stomach rolled as if a herd of buffalo was on stampede. Flynn nudged his shoulder, and he released a sigh.

With a wide grin, Pastor Van Buren began the ceremony. He spoke of the importance of God in their marriage, how they could face anything with the three of them together. He talked of prayer and communication between each other, then the quoted the Bible verse about not letting the sun go down on anger. A few more words, then he led them in their vows. Moments later, he announced, "Mr. and Mrs. Ewan McKay," and the congregation applauded.

The most serious event in his life, and it was over in a trice. They had a two o'clock train, so their time at the reception would be limited. He hoped Daria wouldnae be disappointed. They made their way outside where the ladies had set up a buffet line.

Eyes wide and face pale, Daria glanced at him. "I couldn't eat a thing."

"Me neither." He smiled and tucked her hand into the crook of his arm. "Let's mingle with our guests for wee bit, then you can change clothes for the journey. I'll make your excuses. Perhaps we'll be ready to eat after we've been on the train."

Relief danced across her features. "Thank you. I feel badly not partaking of this spread that Rayne worked so hard to organize."

"Today is all about you, so don't give it another thought. Besides, she seemed to revel in the challenge."

Time passed in a blur. Daria began to wilt, and Ewan pulled out his pocket watch. His heart pounded. Another hour, and he'd be alone with this gorgeous woman. Well, alone in a crowd of other passengers.

Wrapping an arm around her waist, he whispered in her ear, "Time to go." He nodded to the couple they'd been talking to. "Thank you for coming and stay as long as you'd like. There is still a groaning board of food."

The couple moved away, and Daria sagged against him. "Who knew having fun could be so exhausting."

He chuckled, then gestured to Rayne and jerked his head toward the church. She rushed over and took Daria from him. He gestured toward Mr. Ilbert's carriage. "I'll wait there. The bags are already at the station." Watching them go, he swallowed past the lump in his throat. A bittersweet day. He wouldn't have met Daria if he'd stayed in Scotland, but it would have been nice to marry her in his homeland. He'd take her there someday. When Mr. Nesmith, the attorney in Scotland, had proven Father's innocence.

In less time than he thought possible, Daria appeared outside. Although she'd swapped her fancy gown for a simple white blouse and brown skirt, she looked just as lovely. She met his gaze over the heads of the congregants, and her face pinked. She seemed to blush at the smallest provocation, and he enjoyed bringing color to her cheeks.

She threaded her way through the mob to him, then waved at Rayne who stood on the steps.

Bowing, he took her hand in his, then straightened and winked. "Your chariot awaits, m'lady." As anticipated, her porcelain skin took on a rosy hue.

After a deep curtsy, she gave him a saucy smile. "Thank you, m'lord." Giggling, she let him help her into the conveyance.

The door closed, and they were alone. His heart pounded in his ears, and his mouth dried. He suddenly felt like a schoolboy in short pants, awkward and unsure. Shaking his head, he gave himself a mental slap. What was wrong with him? He'd met nobility in drawing rooms. *He'd* been nobility.

"A penny for your thoughts." Daria cocked her head. "Are you regretting your decision to marry?"

"Not at all." He cradled her cold hands in his and rubbed her fingers. "Never. Frankly, I was at a loss for words."

"Surprising for a lawyer in training."

"Mr. Ilbert would be disappointed." He laughed. "The formality of it all...I don't know..."

"Adds a strangeness. I felt it too. But now it's just us again, in our everyday clothes." She sighed. "It was nice of Mr. Ilbert to give us this time to go to Rhode Island."

"He wants to see things put right for you." Ewan patted his pocket. "And he gave us a very generous traveling allowance."

"Our boss is a good man. I can see why you chose to work for him."

"I'm lucky he was willing to take me, stained reputation and all." Ewan rubbed the back of his neck. "Which is why I knew he'd let us follow the trail back East. He's like a terrier with a bone in his search for the truth. I often wonder if he has his own story of injustice, but I daren't ask."

"No, he's a private man." She shifted on the seat and bumped his shoulder. "But I do sense a certain something, which is why I do little things for him. He seems to need...tending."

Tingles spread down his back, and he gazed at her face. *Thank You, Lord, for providing this woman. She is lovely to look at, but more importantly, she has a gentle and giving heart. None but her would be able to see past Mr. Ilbert's gruff manner. She has been through the fire, but isn't bitter. Rather she looks for ways to serve and build up others. She has burrowed her way into my heart.*

Would Daria grow to love him as a husband despite his copious faults and shortcomings?

Chapter Seventeen

Leaning back in the plush seat, Daria gazed out the window at the changing landscape. The journey to Wyoming in second class had been nice, but the first-class compartment Mr. Ilbert paid for contained long-forgotten luxury. The wood and brass fixtures gleamed. Burgundy-colored velvet cushions enveloped her. Lights shimmered in the sconces, casting a cheery glow over her.

She smothered a yawn. Despite the comfort of the train and its sleeping compartments, she'd barely slept last night. Her mind replayed the wedding, reception, and meal in the dining car. Ewan had been solicitous and attentive. Keeping the conversation light, he'd entertained her with stories of his growing-up years. They'd laughed well into the evening until she'd suddenly folded with fatigue. But after lying down, her thoughts tumbled and pushed against each other.

This morning he greeted her with a smile, again keeping her occupied. Did he realize how nervous she was about what would happen in Rhode Island? Even if the courts decided in her favor, she couldn't count on Amaryllis to go away quietly. She would somehow make herself appear the victim, the grieving widow. Had she ever loved Father? Daria's chin trembled.

Ewan patted her hand. "Would you like to get something to eat?"

"Trying to divert my attention again?" Daria lifted one slender shoulder in a half-hearted shrug. "Train travel is faster than coach, but there is still too much time to think."

"Mr. Ilbert wouldn't have sent us if he didn't believe the case ready to win." He squeezed her fingers. "Besides, this is giving us the opportunity to get even more acquainted."

"There is that." She sent him an appreciative smile. "You were quite a scamp as a boy."

"Aye. My parents earned every one of their gray hairs. "Come, I'm starving."

He guided her through the cars, his hand lightly resting on her hip. The warmth of his touch seeped through her dress, and she shivered.

They arrived at the dining car, and the porter met them at the door. "Good afternoon, sir, ma'am." He bowed. "We're right full at the moment. Do you mind sharing a table?"

"Not at all." Ewan nodded.

"Thank you, sir." He led them to a table where a well-dressed, middle-aged man and woman perused the menu. "Mr. and Mrs. McKay, this is Mr. and Mrs. Hall."

The couple looked up, and the man rose. "Thank you for joining us."

Daria narrowed her eyes. They seemed familiar, but perhaps her anxiety was making her imagine things.

Mr. Hall seated himself. "No need for formality. Please call us Eleanor and Alfred."

Ewan nodded. "I'm Ewan, and this is my wife, Daria."

"Daria. An unusual name." Eleanor studied her. "I knew one many years ago. A young girl in Rhode Island."

A chill swept over Daria. "I'm from Newport. We're returning there on...uh...family business."

Eleanor gaped at her. "Was your father Lewis Burke?"

Tears filled Daria's eyes, and she pressed one hand against her heart. "Yes. That's him. He died."

"You poor dear." She glanced at her husband. "That's when we lost contact with your family. We're still in Newport, but Amaryllis didn't seem to want much to do with your father's friends. We'd heard you left town, but no one knew why." She beamed at Daria and Ewan. "I should have guessed it was to marry. How did you two meet?"

Ewan nudged her shoulder and grinned. "Through the Westward Home and Hearts Matrimonial Agency, and I couldnae have picked a more perfect bride myself."

Daria ducked her head as her cheeks heated. Was he putting on a show for the couple, or did he honestly believe his words?

Alfred cocked his head. "I've seen the advertisements, but never met anyone who actually used the service. You seem quite happy."

The waiter arrived for their order, and Daria swallowed a sigh of relief. Yes, she was happy, but was it in the way the Halls thought? Blissfully wedded?

After the man left, Eleanor cleared her throat and said, "I don't mean to pry, but you're returning for family business. Is everything all right?"

Ewan held up a hand. "We're not at liberty to discuss the situation."

"A court case, perhaps?" Alfred lifted one eyebrow. "I have a friend who is an attorney, and he uses that phrase often."

"I'm afraid so."

Eleanor's eyes widened. "Unsurprising. I don't want to gossip, but from what I've heard, your stepmother has been trying to marry off her girls to the rich and famous. She didn't have much luck with those in Newport who recognize her social-climbing ways, and she's turned her sights to English nobility. Who knows what she's done to attract their attention."

Alfred laid his hand on his wife's arm. "Eleanor..."

"What? I'm not telling tales." Eleanor shook off his hand. "It's true. And last week, Pansy was caught kissing the fiancé of another young woman. Shameful. Her sister, Magnolia, is it? She's not too bad, seems to be ruled by the two of them, but none can be trusted. Your father would be so disappointed."

Daria's heart pounded. These people knew her father. Remembered his goodness. "Did you know my mother, too?"

"Yes, she was a delight." Eleanor frowned. "Lewis was devastated when she died. She meant everything to him."

Ewan gave Daria a one-armed hug, then extended his hand to Alfred. "How fortuitous to run into you. I'm sure it means a lot to Daria to meet people who knew her parents." He glanced at her. "May we call on you as character witnesses, if necessary?"

"Absolutely. We'll do anything to help Lewis's daughter." Alfred shook his hand. "You can't discuss the case, but I'd hazard a guess that Amaryllis has manipulated things to take what isn't hers."

"How did you...?"

He rubbed his jaw. "I'm in the insurance business. I recognize her type."

Their food arrived, and they ate their fill, chatting about inconsequential topics. Daria pushed aside her empty plate. Was the Halls presence coincidence? Had God arranged for them to be on their train? Did He work that closely in people's lives?

Eleanor wiped her mouth and climbed to her feet. "This has been lovely. I hope to see you again before we arrive."

Alfred stood, then reached into his pocket and handed Ewan an ivory-colored embossed card. "Please contact me should you require

Eleanor or I to speak on Daria's behalf. We'd be delighted to help." He took his wife's arm, and they made their way down the aisle out of the car.

Ewan huffed out a deep breath, then finger-combed his hair. "The chances are slim meeting your father's friends was happenstance. I'd say God has been working on the situation on our behalf, wouldn't you?"

"Definitely, and I'm humbled. Why would He do that?"

"Because He loves you, lass. He wants to bless His children."

"He could do that without returning my wealth."

"Aye, and that's not certain at this stage, but He's with us, and that's all that matters."

Her heart warmed. She sagged against the seat. "Would you mind if I turned in for the night? I'm suddenly quite worn out."

"Understandable, lass." He rose and helped her to her feet. They wended their way through the cars until they came to her sleeping compartment.

The train lurched, thrusting her against him. She could feel his heart pounding in his chest. Or was that hers? Her cheeks heated as his arms came around her. His face inches away, his eyes pierced hers, his pupils dilating. His breath brushed her skin, and his gaze flicked to her mouth.

Her pulse skittered as he lowered his head and pressed his lips to hers.

Chapter Eighteen

Heart thudding against his ribs, Ewan reveled at the feel of Daria's lips on his, timid at first, then responding with suppressed passion. Her arms snaked around his waist. She fit perfectly within his embrace, her form soft and supple. Their breath mingled.

Then she was gone.

He opened his eyes. She stood against the wall of the corridor, one hand over her mouth. Her face was blotchy, her gaze downcast. Was she embarrassed or repulsed? No, not disgusted. Her reaction said as much. Was it possible she was beginning to care for him? Love him as a wife loves a husband? Even in the dim light, her porcelain skin shone and her honey-gold hair shimmered.

"Daria, look at me." He pitched his voice low, soothing, speaking as he would to a skittish horse. "I'm sorry for taking liberties. It was improper of me to kiss you here, in the hallway."

She lifted her head, but her gaze focused on his chin. "It is me who should apologize." Her hand fumbled for the latch on the compartment door. "I...uh...don't know what came over me."

"There's nothing to be ashamed of. We're husband and wife." A stray lock of hair had come free from its pins, and he tucked the silky tress behind her ear. She trembled under his touch. "Granted, displays of affection in public are frowned upon, but not as scandalous as in the past. We're married. Kissing is not only okay"—he grinned—"it's expected."

"But we don't love each other, not that way." Her eyes clouded. "Not yet."

His face fell. "That's true, and I'm sorry to have offended you."

The wooden door slid open behind her, and she dropped her hand to her side. "I'm not offended. It's just...I don't know...I'm not ready."

"I understand." He sighed. "Good night, Daria. Sleep well."

"You, too." She gave him a feeble smile and ducked into the alcove, then closed the door, the curtain-covered window blocking his view inside. The lock clicked, loud and final.

Ewan rubbed the back of his neck and huffed out another sigh. He'd rushed her. What had he been thinking? He hadn't been thinking. That was the problem. She'd been so close that he could see the flecks of violet in her blue eyes, and he'd fallen into them. Inches away, her lips looked so soft, inviting. Calling to him.

Did she know how beguiling she was? How beautiful? Not vixen-like, but demure and unassuming. He'd have preferred to pull the pins from her hair and let it cascade down her back rather than tuck the errant strand behind her ear. Someday. Would it be soon?

He scrubbed at his face with cold fingers, then gave the compartment one last glance before making his way down the narrow corridor. Muffled conversations and laughter filtered through the doors of some of the compartments as he passed, his feet soundless on the lush carpet.

If he wasn't mistaken, she'd shivered at his touch, not shuddered. A vast difference. She seemed affected by his proximity, in a good way. But they needed to finish the case. Put her past to rest, once and for all. To undo the damage that her stepmother and stepsisters had done. To heal the wounds that prevented her from healthy relationships with those around her.

After what she'd experienced, it was a wonder she hadn't entered a convent, a place safe from the manipulations and machinations of the world. Cloistered. Protected.

Could he protect her?

To a point. He could handle some aspects. Follow up on the tasks assigned by Mr. Ilbert. Ferret out information. Ensure her comfort during the journey. But it was her Creator who could truly keep her safe. Wrap her scars in His love and envelope her in peace.

His face fell. He'd been so busy getting everything in order, he'd relied on himself with the occasional prayer tossed heavenward for strength and success. He claimed to be a believer, but his faith had been tenuous at best. There was more at stake than victory in the courtroom, and he needed to petition the One who could take care of Daria better than he could.

Hurrying through the cars, he arrived in first class, found his seat, and sank into the plush cushions. Few passengers remained, presumably either at dinner or retired for the night. He peered out the window at the inky darkness. The train was traveling too fast for him to see any stars, but he caught sight of the moon's sliver above the trees before it disappeared, enveloped by a cloud.

The lurching and bucking he'd experienced in his third-class journey across the continent more than a year ago wasn't evident in the sumptuous first-class accommodations. He could get used to such grandeur. His glance fell to the vacant seat beside him, and he ran his palm across the burgundy velvet. Although Daria slept only a few cars away, he missed her presence. She'd gotten under his skin, found her way into his heart in a matter of weeks. How was that possible?

His reflection stared back at him, grim and foreboding. Caught up in his thoughts, he'd fallen prey to worry. He bowed his head and closed his eyes, shutting out the distractions and man-made opulence. *Oh, Father, thank You for Your patience with me as I fumble my way through each day. Running ahead of You, then beckoning for You to keep up with my plans. My plans, not Yours. Forgive my arrogance at thinking I'm in control. At failing to seek You and Your will in all things. Thank You for bringing Daria into my life. Pave the way for her healing in her mind, soul, and spirit. And please work a miracle that Amaryllis and her daughters see the error of their ways.*

Could a woman such as Daria's stepmother come to the Lord? Doubt pricked his heart, and his face warmed. He shook his head. Seconds after taking the situation to the Father and vowing to trust, he'd allowed uncertainty to edge its way in. Daria deserved a man of deeper faith. Could he grow to be such a man?

Chapter Nineteen

Brakes squealed, and steam wafted past the windows obscuring the activity on the station platform. Daria clutched her reticule, squinting through the cloud. The train jerked to a stop. Little more than a month had passed since she'd stood here, heart in her throat, embarking on a new life. And now she was back. For better or worse.

Her pulse stuttered, and she swallowed against the unexpected lump in her throat. She hadn't expected the wave of emotion that swept over her at the familiar sights. Her stomach clenched, and she drew a shuddering breath.

Ewan laid his fingers over hers, his thumb drawing circles on the back of her hand. He leaned close to her ear. "You are no longer alone. I will be with you through the entire process. And more importantly, God is here and in charge."

Tears pricked the backs of her eyes. Pressing her lips together, she nodded.

"It is natural to be afraid, but try to rest in Him."

"What if my innocence can't be proved?" She sniffled. "You have personal experience that blameless people go to jail."

A shadow crossed his face. "Let's not borrow trouble."

"I'm sorry. I shouldn't have brought up your father."

"No worries, lass. He's never far from my thoughts." He gave her an encouraging smile. "The sheriff never found the so-called stolen goods, so your stepmother's case is tenuous at best." He rose and helped her to her feet. "Now, we're going to the hotel so you can freshen up, then we'll present ourselves to the court. They will want to know you've arrived."

Her stomach rolled, and she swayed against him. His arm went around her shoulder, his strength keeping her from falling into a sobbing mass on the floor. "Will they keep me? You know, put me in a cell."

"A slim possibility, but doubtful." He kissed her forehead, then bent and pierced her with a look, firm yet gentle. "Everything is going to work out. I don't know how, but it will."

His crystal-blue gaze caressed her. The noise and motion faded away as she stared into his eyes. His kindness and encouraging words smoothed the tightness from her shoulders. She blinked away the moisture from her eyes and straightened her spine. She nodded, and a nervous giggle escaped. "Thank you for...for everything. I couldn't do this without you."

He glanced around the now-vacant car. "It seems we're the last to disembark. Let me help you." He slipped one arm around her waist and guided her down the aisle, then had her wait while he descended the stairs before turning to take her hand. Her heels clicked on the metal steps, then she was on the wooden platform.

Wagons rattled, shouts rang out, and horses whinnied, punctuated by the thump of trunks and crates hitting the ground. Ensconced in the quietude of Wyoming, she'd forgotten the congestion of Newport.

"There's our ride." Ewan pointed to a man holding a small slate with McKay chalked on its surface. "Mr. Ilbert thought of everything."

An hour later, they'd settled into their rooms. Their lavish, palatial rooms. Mr. Ilbert was treating her like a queen rather than a lowly employee. She didn't deserve his esteem. The luggage had been delivered, and she'd taken a bath to wash off the stain of travel. Clothed in her best dress, a simple lavender garment with three-quarter-length sleeves, she'd donned a small white hat with a matching ribbon. The heat was oppressive, and perspiration formed at her hairline.

"Daria. Are you ready?" Ewan's voice was faint from the hallway.

She hurried across the room and opened the door. Her pulse skipped. My, but he looked good in his freshly brushed-gray suit, the jacket nipped in at the waist making his shoulders appear broader than usual. She licked her lips. "Ready."

He winked at her. "You look lovely. Now, remember what Mr. Ilbert told you: never let them see you sweat." He chuckled. "A bit crass, but he's right."

Lifting her chin, she sent him an exaggerated grin.

"Maybe tone it down a wee bit." He chuckled. "But you've got the idea."

They descended to the lobby, then out of the hotel where a carriage awaited. She gaped at him. "I didn't realize Mr. Ilbert was going to take care of so much for me. He's spending a fortune."

"He has it to spend, and he said he wants to leave nothing to chance." Ewan helped her into the conveyance, and a short time later they arrived at the courthouse. In the dimness of the carriage he turned toward her. "I'd like to pray before we go in."

Tears threatened, and she nodded. How could she be happy and tearful at the same time? This man evoked such unfamiliar emotions. Was she beginning to care for him as a wife should? She closed her eyes as his words filled the carriage, petitioning their heavenly Father to work all things for good. She remembered that verse. It had been one of her earthly father's favorites, but she'd forgotten. She'd allowed the difficulties and mistreatment to push the verse from her mind. *Whatever You decide needs to happen, God, I will obey.*

Peace wrapped around her, like one of her mother's quilts, and she sighed. With Ewan and God by her side, she could face her enemies. No matter what transcended, the battle was already won. She hoped the Lord's plans didn't include jail, but she would acquiesce. How would Ewan react if she was found guilty? Would he stand by her or initiate a divorce? He could request an annulment since they hadn't consummated the marriage. She nibbled her lower lip. *Dear God, it will break my heart if he leaves me.*

They entered the imposing brick building, and Ewan survey the lobby teeming with people, seemingly more than the number living in Rocky Mountain Springs. He hated crowds. Beside him, Daria gasped, and her hand on his arm tightened to a grip. He followed her gaze. Ah, the stepmother and her daughters.

Dressed as if attending a ball, the woman and her daughters wore watered-silk gowns edged with lace, Amaryllis in scarlet, and the girls in emerald green and cobalt blue. Their hair was swept into elaborate styles and adorned with flowers. The woman had aged well, her complexion radiant and smooth-looking. Even the skin at her neck wasn't crepey. At first glance, she was an attractive woman. Then she turned and met his gaze, her expression severe and her eyes dark and glittering. Her eyebrow lifted as her stare slid to Daria at his side.

She marched toward them, mouth set in a slash. Her daughters scurried behind her like a pair of puppies. Fisting her hands on her hips, she stopped in front of them. "Well, the prodigal child returns. You think you can get away with stealing from me and your sisters, your own family. You'll get your comeuppance."

Before Daria could say anything, he moved in front of her, blocking her from the nasty woman. Pulling himself to his full height, he glared at her. "Madam, I'll thank you not to speak to my wife in that manner."

"Your wife?" Sarcasm dripped from her words. "Shame on you for not checking her out before marrying this guttersnipe. She's—"

"Enough!" He held up his hand, and she nearly swallowed her lips. "In addition to being my wife, she is also my client, and I don't believe the courts would look too kindly on you verbally attacking the defendant in your case."

"Client?" Her jaw dropped.

He had finally rendered her speechless. "We'll see you inside, madam. Good day." He bowed and swept away, Daria on his arm. He turned toward her and dropped one eyelid in a slow wink, provoking the desired reaction: she snickered, and relief danced across her features. He led her into the courtroom and gestured to a pair of vacant seats.

As they sat, she gulped and said, "Are all these people here for my case? I don't know them."

The door to the back opened, and Amaryllis and her daughters shuffled in. Daria's stepmother held a lace-edged handkerchief to her mouth, and her face was streaked with tears, looking nothing like the harridan who'd shot verbal barbs at them moments ago. Apparently, her tactics were going to include playing the distraught victim. Interesting.

"No. The judge will hear many motions today. You are here because your stepmother's attorney is going to ask that you be jailed or to set a very high bail for you."

Her cheeks went white.

He patted her arm, then jerked his head to a beefy-looking man with hair the color of a new penny, and who looked better suited to working as a bodyguard than an attorney. Ewan nodded to the man. "But the attorney over there has been retained by Mr. Ilbert to prevent that from happening. And the expression on his face leads me to believe we're in good hands."

"He does appear...confident."

A light breeze ruffled the curtains at the window and sent the crisp soapy smell from Daria's hair wafting into his nose. He stifled the urge to take a deep breath to inhale her clean essence. The poor girl must be terrified, her future in the hands of a selfish, manipulative woman who very well could have bribed or at least influenced the judge. He had no proof, but money had brought down many a court official.

He gave a sidelong glance at Daria's stepmother. Her regal bearing and expression of disdain reminded him of the upper crust he'd seen at home. The English who thought they were better than the Scotch and the Irish. As if their blood ran blue instead of red like common folk.

She was a climber. That fact was irrefutable, with her taking Daria's inheritance and trying to marry off her girls to the highest bidders. She apparently also had a mean streak evidenced by her claims of Daria's thievery. Sadly, the woman didn't understand that true riches lay in heaven. Well, she'd taken on the wrong people, and justice would prevail. *Please God.*

Chapter Twenty

The following day, Ewan sauntered along the shore with Daria, a basket of food on one arm. As anticipated, Mr. Wilson, the attorney retained by Mr. Ilbert, had been eloquent, convincing the judge that having traveled nearly two thousand miles, Daria was hardly a flight risk. She'd not been arrested, and proof had not been found of her guilt, yet she'd come of her own accord to defend the charge of thievery. He also intimated that Amaryllis might be the recipient of charges in the future. The judge had disallowed the comment, reprimanding Wilson about speculation, but the attorney's point had been made. With his next breath, Judge Ellis agreed there was no reason to incarcerate Daria and told them to return in one week to try the case. With flick of his wrist he waved them from the room.

A salty breeze tugged at his Stetson and stroked his cheeks. He inhaled deeply, relishing the briny aroma he grown up with in Scotland. Rockier than the creamy sand beaches of his homeland, the Newport shoreline was peppered with boulders. As he ambled beside Daria, he glanced at the occasional mansion they passed, massive opulent houses the rich has constructed as summer cottages.

The town was an intriguing hodgepodge of modest colonial-era homes and ostentatious manor homes reminiscent of those he'd seen in Glasgow. Buildings that could hold the population of a small village. Buildings just like the one he'd grown up in.

He gritted his teeth and shoved his empty hand into his pocket. Seeing the homes tore at his heart. It wasn't the loss of wealth that clawed at him, but the knowledge that Da was languishing in prison while he strolled free. He hadn't heard from Mr. Nesmith nigh on three months. Had the man given up the fight? Was there no hope?

"Are you all right, Ewan?" Daria laid a hand on his arm to stay his movement. "You seem upset."

"Too many memories." He jerked his head toward the white Italianate villa she'd told him belonged to a New York clothing magnate. "Not that our home looked like this or any of the others we've walked by, but the immense size brings to mind my boyhood home, reminding me that Da is still in jail."

"I'm so sorry." Her forehead creased. "You've not heard from the attorney?"

"No." He shifted the basket from one hand to the other. "I'm sorry. I didnae mean to ruin the mood. Besides, this trip is about you, not me."

"Nonsense. Our loved ones are never far from our thoughts. I'll continue to pray that the situation remedies itself. After he's been released, we should ask him to come to America and live with us. Would you like that?"

He gaped at her. "You wouldn't mind having him in the house?"

"Of course not." She gave him a saucy smile. "Your father and I have much in common: we've both been unjustly accused."

"Let's settle here for our picnic." He chuckled, then gestured to a grassy knoll. "I'm glad to see you more at ease about the case." He set down the basket, and she spread the blanket she'd been carrying. With a flourish, he opened the lid and laid out the food the hotel had prepared for them. Fragrant aromas of fried chicken, potato salad, yeasty rolls, and corn mingled with the sea air.

"Being here has helped." She swept her arm toward the sparkling grayish-blue ocean where white-capped waves crashed onto the shore. "I used to come here early in the morning...before...the vastness of the water always reminds me of God's sovereignty. A short walk would always set my heart at rest, then I could start my day."

"Was it awful?" His heart clenched. "Wait...if you came here, you must have lived nearby."

She pointed at a limestone Victorian in the distance. Surrounded by gardens, the mansion soared four stories into the cloudless sky.

"You must miss it." He returned the container of chicken to the basket. "I didn't think to ask where the house was when I suggested we take a walk along the ocean. We can find somewhere else to picnic."

"I miss Father and Mother, not the house." She forked an ear of corn onto her plate. "I don't need a mansion to be happy. Father believed our true treasure lies in eternity with God, and he passed that belief to me."

"Good thing." He cocked his head and grinned, then pulled out the chicken. "You've seen the tiny abode I'm renting in Rocky Mountain Springs. There's barely enough room for me."

She flushed, and her face glowed as she giggled and helped herself to more food.

He studied her from under his eyebrows. Her parents must have been salt-of-the-earth-type people. Surrounded by great wealth in a mansion along the Rhode Island shore, yet instilling a deep, abiding faith that had nothing to do with money and its accoutrements. Did she know how much of a *treasure* she was?

They sat in companionable silence, munching the succulent delicacies and watching the gulls swoop overhead.

"Well, isn't this cozy."

Daria cringed, and Ewan whipped his head toward the voice. He frowned, his food turning to a lump in his stomach.

Pansy minced toward them, holding a gauzy parasol over her head. Dressed in a white-sprigged muslin dress with a plunging neckline and cap sleeves, she wore an obsequious smile. "It's lovely to see you, Daria. We didn't get to speak before...in court."

Ewan climbed to his feet and stood close to the young woman, forcing her to look up rather than down her nose at him as she had been. A tactic Mr. Ilbert had taught him. "I warned you and your mother about speaking to Daria before the case is settled. You shouldnae be here."

Uncertainty clouded her eyes. "I just wanted to say I'm sorry for all that has happened. She didn't deserve it...what Mother did."

He searched her face, and she held his gaze. Daria's stepsister was a bold one. Was she truly sorry, or was she ingratiating herself in the event that Daria would be found innocent and receive a large portion of inheritance?

"We appreciate you coming by, but you shoudnae be speaking with us. The judge might take a dim view of a conversation outside the courtroom. However, with the information we have, the case should be resolved quickly, and then you can spend time with Daria if you wish."

The young woman pursed her lips into a pout. "You don't have to be rude. I was out for a walk and happened upon you."

Daria rose and stood beside him. "Ewan's not being impolite. He's trying to protect us, so thank you for stopping, but you must do as he says and be on your way. Your presence could create complications."

"Fine." Pansy nodded and turned away, gliding along the path, her skirts swaying as she walked.

Ewan huffed out a loud breath. "That was interesting. Do you think this was truly happenstance?"

"With Pansy? Doubtful." She wrung her hands. "Could this jeopardize my case?"

He cradled her fists in his hands. "I don't know...probably not. If it comes up, we'll give our side of the story and leave the decision to the judge. Now, let's enjoy our lunch and forget about the case for a while. God has a plan and has already gone ahead of us to lay out the solution.

Did God's strategy include Daria being found innocent?

Chapter Twenty-One

Angry gray clouds scudded across the sky as Daria hurried down the sidewalk next to Ewan. The ever-present aroma of salty air mingled with the musky odors of animals, manure, and perspiration. How had she forgotten the overpowering smells of Newport?

People pushed past, jostling her as they hurried to their destinations, eyes averted. Unlike Rocky Mountain Springs, no one smiled or acknowledged her. She searched the crowd for a familiar face, but found none.

Ewan stopped in front of a carved wooden door with an opaque window. Harry Wilson, Attorney at Law was etched on the glass in gold. They went inside, and Daria froze as she stepped onto plush moss-green carpet. With cherrywood shelves filled with leather volumes and upholstered furniture, the room resembled her father's study, even though this office held two desks rather than one. Memories of being curled up on the couch with a book while he hunched over paperwork assailed her.

The young men seated at the desks looked up, and the dark-haired clerk rose. He wiped his ink-stained fingers with a handkerchief as he nodded. "Mr. and Mrs. McKay?"

Daria gulped. Would she ever get used to the title? To being a wife?

"Yes." Ewan cupped her elbow. "We have an appointment."

"Mr. Wilson is expecting you." The clerk gestured toward a door at the back of the room. "This way, please."

Blinking, she shook away the thought and followed the young man to the office where he rapped on the frame, then opened the door. "Mr. and Mrs. McKay have arrived, sir."

She entered another room as luxurious as the first, although a fraction of the size. Sunlight streamed across the attorney's desk through large windows that provided a view of the busy street outside. Was the man as successful as his attire in the courtroom and his opulent office suggested?

Her stomach fluttered as if a chipmunk ran amok inside her belly. The man was hired to help her. Why was she so nervous? She'd allowed her worries to overtake the peace she'd felt after Ewan's prayer. God must think her a fickle woman. One minute claiming deep faith in His plans for her life, and the next, wringing her hands, expecting the worst.

Ewan held her chair, and she lowered herself onto the gorgeous needlepoint cushion. He sat beside her and cleared his throat.

Mr. Wilson smiled and pointed to several sheets of paper covered in precise writing. "I'm just finishing up our plan of attack. Would you care for some tea?"

"No, thank you." Daria shook her head. She couldn't trust that'd she could keep anything down.

"All right. Give me another moment, and we'll discuss our strategy."

She nodded, and Ewan patted her hand, giving her an encouraging glance. He'd been kind to her from the beginning, never once showing frustration or agitation, even after the nightmare of Amaryllis's charges against her disrupted their lives. He'd yet to swerve from his belief that the case would be dismissed, and she would receive her due inheritance.

Oh, that she could have such stalwart faith.

Would God grant her success? Would she inherit Father's wealth, thrusting her back into society as a woman of means? Did she want the house with its collection of happy and sad memories? Was there any reason to stay in Newport? Her life now lay in Wyoming.

Nibbling her lower lip, she peeked at Ewan. How would he feel about her prosperity after his own being stripped? Would he resent her affluence? Maybe she should take a portion as a nest egg and distribute the rest to those in need. Should she give a fragment to Amaryllis despite her awful behavior? Father loved her and would want his wife and her daughters provided for.

Her heart clenched. She didn't want to be generous with them, not after how they'd acted toward her.

Forgive, My child, the soft voice invaded her thoughts.

She cast a look at the ceiling as if expecting to see God's face shining down at her. *But they stole from me and treated me like a servant. No, less than a servant.*

Forgive, the voice repeated.

A deep sigh escaped, and she dropped her gaze to her hands. *Yes, Lord.*

Mr. Wilson laid down his pen and rubbed his hands together. "We've had a Pinkerton agent keeping an eye on your stepmother and her daughters, and their activities have been less than aboveboard. We've also ascertained that the copy of the will she claims is the last your father wrote is a fake. The signature is a forgery. A good one, but phony, nonetheless."

She gaped at him. "Can you prove that?"

"Absolutely. Your father was a businessman and, as such, signed copious documents. Therefore, we have a vast number of signatures to compare to the decree. We have two experts who will be put on the stand if we don't settle this out of court."

"You can do that?"

"Yes, if your stepmother is amenable." He lifted an eyebrow. "That remains to be seen. We don't want to reveal all our cards, but we can indicate to her that we've found *irregularities* with the document. Her attorney should understand what we're saying and advise her to go away quietly unless you wish to press charges against her."

"I-I don't know." Her gaze ricocheted from the attorney to Ewan and back again. "This is a lot to take in."

"I understand. We have several days before the judge needs to be notified whether the case will be proceeding." He rose and opened the door. "Meanwhile, there is a separate case I need to discuss with Mr. McKay." He rose and opened the door. "Randall, would you please settle Mrs. McKay in the waiting area, and get her anything she requires."

Daria rose and turned to the attorney. "Thank you for your help. I'll consider what you've said and let you know."

"Excellent."

As the door closed, Ewan's voice floated toward her. "I love her and—"

Randall motioned to the Prussian-Blue upholstered sofa, and she nearly stumbled. Ewan loved her? Why hadn't he said anything to her? Was he waiting for her to declare herself? Or was he telling the attorney what he thought the man should hear? As a married couple, wouldn't they be expected to love each other? Her stomach quivered at the thought.

Leaning forward, Ewan propped his elbows on his knees. "I love her and must protect her. Is your proof irrefutable? You don't seem the kind of attorney to give false hope to his client, but I must be sure she willnae get hurt."

Mr. Wilson steepled his fingers and leaned back in the chair. "Ironclad. And you're correct about my style. I tell all my clients exactly what they're facing. That way they are prepared for every contingency." He cocked his head. "I understand from Mr. Ilbert that Daria is your mail-order bride. How well do you know her? Did you correspond before marrying?"

Ewan sat up. "Today's the twenty-seventh? She stepped off the train six weeks ago today. We didnae have an opportunity to write letters. Her situation had reached a crisis point, and Miss Crenshaw, the owner of the matrimonial agency, was the liaison and made the arrangements through telegrams."

"Yet you attest to love her after such a short time. Be honest." The attorney narrowed his eyes. "I must know the truth if I'm to do my best by her."

"I do love her." Ewan swallowed. If the warmth of his face was any indication, he must be as red as a sugar beet. "I dinnae know how, but I've managed to fall in love in a month and a half."

With a chuckle, Mr. Wilson shrugged. "I've seen love overtake a man quicker than that. My brother-in-law claims it was love at first sight with my sister." He smiled. "She seems a lovely young woman. Such a shame she's had so much heartache and difficulty in her life. Does she reciprocate your feelings?"

Pulse racing, Ewan rubbed the back of his neck. "I dinnae know. We've developed a camaraderie, and she seems to care for me, but as more of a friend..." He brushed lint from his pants and repeated, "I dinnae know."

"Don't despair." The attorney grinned. "I see how she looks at when your attention is elsewhere. She's smitten."

"You wouldnae play with a man's emotions, would you, sir?"

"Absolutely not."

Blowing out a deep breath, Ewan sagged in the chair. She was growing to love him? How had he not seen that? What if Mr. Wilson couldn't prove the documents false? Thus far, the items Daria was supposed to have stolen hadn't shown up in her possession, but what if Amaryllis figured out a way to plant the evidence in Daria's room at the hotel? What if the judge was crooked?

His gaze shot around the room, taking in the gleaming shelves crammed with law books, tastefully arranged furniture, and framed newsprints with headlines that shouted success. Mr. Wilson was obviously good at what he did. One of the best, according to Mr. Ilbert. Did God have a hand in selecting the attorney here in Newport? Was He that closely involved in the case?

Ewan pressed his lips together. After all the encouragement he gave to Daria last night, he should have more faith. The Lord must be tired of his erratic trust. Believing in His sovereignty one moment and panicking the next. Taking matters into his own hands. Trying to win on his own merits.

Relying on anyone other than God was foolishness. He'd made that mistake in Scotland, and things didnae work out for the best. He'd promised himself a new start in America, and he was falling prey to his old tendencies.

"You seem to be arguing with yourself, Mr. McKay." The attorney sent him a wry smile. "Who's winning?"

With a snort, Ewan shook his head. "It's a bad habit, and I dinnae know at the moment. Are you a man of faith, Mr. Wilson?"

"Yes, I am. I take it from your question that you are, too?"

"Aye, but it's been wavering of late. I know I'm to trust in the good Lord and His plans, but this case has tried my steadfastness."

"As often happens when the stakes are so high."

"Aye." Ewan finger-combed his hair. "Would He bring us this far to you and the proof you've unearthed, only to allow Daria to be somehow declared guilty?" He pierced the man with his gaze. "I can't lose her, Mr. Wilson, not after I've just found her."

Chapter Twenty-Two

Footsteps echoing on the wooden floor, Daria marched down the aisle of the courtroom and slid into the curved bench next to Mr. Wilson. Ewan dropped beside her, sending her an encouraging smile. Her toes curled, and warmth filled her. He'd been the Rock of Gibraltar these last few days, and she wouldn't have made it this far without him.

Talking among themselves, men and women began to fill the room. Amaryllis and her daughters had yet to make an appearance. Despite Mr. Wilson's efforts to settle the case out of court for lack of evidence, her stepmother maintained that the will was genuine, and Daria had stolen several pieces of jewelry and stock certificates from her before leaving for Wyoming.

What did her stepmother have planned? Moisture sprang out on Daria's palms, and she wiped her hands on her skirt as she glanced around the large space. Sunlight poured in through the massive floor-to-ceiling, twelve-over-twelve windows. The ebony-colored judge's bench rose slightly above the walnut-wood seating that circled three-quarters of the room. Constructed before the American Revolution, the Georgian-style building had witnessed scores of historic events.

The door opened. Amaryllis, Magnolia, and Pansy swept into the room like royalty, dressed in their usual silks and satins, and hair piled in ornate styles. Their attorney, a short, beefy man, followed on their heels. He clutched an overstuffed leather satchel in one hand while mopping his flushed, perspiring face with a white handkerchief with the other hand. Like his briefcase, his suit bulged in several places. His balding pate glistened. He appeared an absentminded buffoon until his piercing gray eyes met hers, exuding intelligence and confidence bordering on arrogance.

Her pulse tripped, and nausea threatened to overwhelm her. She swallowed against the lump that formed in her throat, her breath coming in small gasps. Ewan reached for her hand, and laced his fingers in hers, his thumb rubbing circles on her skin. A display that was highly improper in public but soothed her racing heart. She could do this. She *would* do this. Not that she had much choice, but she would not embarrass herself or Ewan by falling apart.

They'd prayed together after breakfast, and she'd been at peace until they'd arrived at the courthouse—the impressive two-story brick building soaring above her. The Declaration of Independence had been read aloud from the front steps only days after being adopted by the colonies. She'd hesitated, wondering about the future of her own freedom, then Ewan had led her inside.

A man strode into the center of the room. "All rise!"

Conversation ceased as the crowd climbed to its feet.

Black robe swirling around his legs, Judge Ellis entered through a side door, then stalked to the bench. He lowered himself into the chair, and the bailiff gestured for the occupants to sit before moving to the right-hand side of the judge.

Ewan patted her arm, then folded his hands in his lap.

"First case: Burke versus McKay." The bailiff's voice echoed against the wood paneling.

Amaryllis's attorney jumped to his feet and approached the bench. "Begging the court's pardon, but we're withdrawing our complaint."

The judge's face darkened, and his eyebrows came together in a deep scowl. "What?"

"We recognize that this is very last minute, but it is only moments ago that we come to believe the will in our possession is fraudulent. A very good forgery, mind you, rendering Mrs. Burke the victim here. She would never have taken the bequest had she known the document was counterfeit, and we will be pursuing how this unfortunate situation came to be."

Daria goggled at the man as Ewan gave a derisive snort. Mr. Wilson looked pleased and not the least bit surprised. Her gaze shot from the judge, whose mouth was set in a thin slash, to Amaryllis, who pressed a lace-edged hanky against her mouth, a single tear trickling down her cheek. Crocodile tears, no doubt. Daria's stepsisters wore impassive expressions.

"Case dismissed." Judge Ellis banged the gavel on the table with a resounding crack. "The next time you waste my time, Mr. Manley, there will be consequences. Is that understood?"

"Yes, sir." The attorney nodded and pivoted, motioning for Amaryllis and her daughters to precede him from the room.

"What just happened?" Daria stared at Mr. Wilson.

He put a finger to his lips and jerked his head toward the back of the room. As one, they got up and tiptoed from the room.

In the wide corridor, voices surrounded her, people rushed past, footsteps clattering, and periodic laughter split the air. Mr. Wilson led her to the far corner and bent his head. "Amaryllis's attorney finally convinced her of the futility of her case. He's walking a fine line of ethics by claiming she knew nothing about the will being a fake, but unless you'd like to bring suit against her, the courts will accept her statement."

Ewan cocked his head. "So the original document filed with the clerk stands?"

"Yes." Mr. Wilson glanced at Daria. "Are you aware of the will's contents, Mrs. McKay?"

"No. Father never discussed them with me, other than to say he would ensure I would always be taken care of."

"I can assure you that he did." Mr. Wilson shrugged. "It's a bit inappropriate to discuss in the hallway, and we'll need to arrange a meeting with your stepmother and the other beneficiaries, but I want you to know the house is yours, and your father set up a trust for you that has a significant balance. Mrs. Burke receives an allowance, but if my intelligence is correct, she has nearly drained the account."

Daria gasped. "What will happen to her?"

"Unless you see fit to support her, she may end up in the poorhouse."

"Serves her right." Ewan glowered at the attorney. "She's done nothing but bring heartache to Daria."

"Ewan, we mustn't think that way." Daria laid her hand on his arm. "I can scarcely take in this information, but one thing is for certain, God has worked out the circumstances as we asked, so we must thank Him."

He ducked his head. "As always, you're right. It's hard not to bear a grudge. I see what kind of woman she is, and she deserves to be punished."

"Perhaps, but God shows us mercy, and we should consider doing the same. I don't know what that looks like at the moment, but we should give serious consideration to how we will respond."

"You are a kind and gracious lady, Mrs. McKay." Mr. Wilson bowed. "Your parents would be pleased."

"And hopefully my Lord as well, Mr. Wilson."

"Daria, may I have a word?" Amaryllis approached, the usual haughtiness absent from her expression. Was she truly sorry for the ill she'd caused, or was her act of graciousness another ploy?

Chapter Twenty-Three

Mouth dry, Daria licked her lips and stared at Amaryllis. Her stepmother's shoulders were slumped, and her face pale and waxen. She clutched her handkerchief in one hand and reached toward Daria with the other. "Please, I'll only take a moment."

Beside her, Ewan stiffened and straightened to his full height. "I hope you've come to ask forgiveness," he growled.

Tears filled Amaryllis's eyes. "I have. My behavior to Daria was unconscionable, and I'd like to make amends." Her gaze slid to Daria. "I don't know how, but I thought we could discuss it, together, just the two of us."

The noise from the crowds faded as Daria's heart rumbled in her ears. All the years of horrible actions, and Amaryllis thought a simple apology would wipe away the hurt? Was the woman that naïve? "I don't know." She sighed. She'd said that a lot over the last few days.

"Please." Amaryllis's voice broke. "I've made arrangements for the girls and me to be out of the house by tomorrow, if that's acceptable. You could come over for tea, and we could...uh...share memories of your father." She shrugged and dropped her head.

Was her stepmother really sorry? Or was she sorry she'd been caught? Or worse, was the invitation part of some plot to get her alone? Daria narrowed her eyes. Amaryllis had never been violent, just mean-spirited with an acidic tongue. The servants would be there, and possibly her stepsisters. "All right. There's no time like the present." She turned to Ewan. "I'll only be an hour or so. Would you work with Mr. Wilson to make arrangements for the reading of the will? I'd like to go home as soon as possible."

His eyes clouded. "Home? To your father's house?"

She laid her hand on his arm. "No, to Wyoming." Like a thunderclap, she'd known as soon as Mr. Wilson informed her the house and its contents belonged to her that she didn't want them, that her home lay with the man next to her. The gentle, generous, and gorgeous man who'd dropped everything to come to Rhode Island. The man she loved. She knew that, too. And he might not love her in return, but she would be the best wife he could want, and perhaps someday he would grow to care for her.

He smiled, his face glowing as if lit from within. "I'll see if we cannae tie things up by the middle of next week, hopefully sooner." He looked at Amaryllis, then back to Daria. "And you'll be okay with her? On your own?"

"I'll be fine."

His expression tight, he nodded. "An hour. No more."

She put her fingers to her forehead in a mock salute. "Aye, sir."

The corner of his mouth lifted, and he chuckled. "Get on with you."

Pivoting on her heel, she glanced at Amaryllis. "I assume you have the carriage?"

"Yes, out front. I had the girls call for it."

"Excellent." Daria's stomach fluttered, and her knees quivered, but she couldn't show Amaryllis her nervousness. And there was no reason for anxiety. She had the courts behind her. But years of learning her stepmother couldn't be trusted was a hard habit to break.

They exited the courthouse and descended the stairs. Sunshine warmed Daria's back and caused her to squint at the brightness. Birds sang and trilled as if they were celebrating with her. The azure sky was cloudless. Somewhere close, a gardenia bloomed, thickening the air with its heady fragrance.

Her father's carriage waited to her left, the glossy-black paint gleaming. She walked to the conveyance and stroked the enameled wood. Memories of snuggling with her father inside the dim recesses washed over her, and tears filled her eyes. She blinked them away, then accepted the footman's assistance to climb inside. She dropped onto the worn, but plush, burgundy-colored cushion, and Amaryllis entered and sat across from her. The door closed, and they were alone. The vehicle lurched forward, and Daria tucked her hands under her skirts.

"Thank you for coming to the house." Amaryllis sighed. "I don't deserve your kindness."

"I'm a believer, Amaryllis. Treating you well despite our...uh...history...is what God expects of me." She cocked her head. "Frankly, I don't trust you, but I'm willing to give you a fair shake. Will the girls be joining us?" She nibbled the inside of her cheek. If so, was that good or bad?

"No, we agreed it was best if you and I settle our differences first."

Several minutes later, the carriage braked in front of her childhood home. Daria peeked out the window and took a deep breath. The scent of salt air seeped into the compartment as she gazed at the pillared, brick, Greek Revival building. Green shutters flanked the windows, and rocking chairs filled the upper balcony. A rainbow of blooms nodded in the breeze on either side of the stairs. The six weeks she'd been gone suddenly felt like a lifetime.

The door opened, and Daria stepped to the ground. Amaryllis joined her, and they entered the house. She surveyed the foyer with the eyes of a stranger. Her father's portrait smiled at her from its gilt frame, and the chandelier sparkled overhead.

"We'll take tea in the parlor, but I thought you'd want to tour the house first."

"I would." She peeked at Amaryllis. How had she transformed from a bitter harridan to the soft-spoken lady beside her?

They wandered through the house, Daria running her fingers along doorposts and across furniture. She studied the oil paintings and watercolors hanging on the papered walls. Each room held at least one bouquet of flowers. They reached the last room, her father's bedroom, and Daria stared at the lavender silk gown lying on the bed. Her mother's dress. She rushed forward and snatched the beautiful garment into her arms and buried her face into the fabric. The dress had been one of her mother's favorites. She raised her head and saw the rest of the gowns, draped on chairs and hanging from the curtain rods. "What—"

The door slammed, and her head whipped around. Amaryllis was gone.

"If I can't have the house, neither can you." Her voice was strident. "Perhaps spending your last moments with your parents' things will bring you some comfort."

Daria dropped the dress and raced to the door. She tugged on the handle. Locked. Of course. She jiggled the knob. "Let me out, Amaryllis. You can't keep me here."

"I don't plan to." Glass shattered, and the smell of lantern oil permeated the room. "You should have left well enough alone, Daria."

Smoke wafted into the room from under the door and curled around Daria's legs.

Chapter Twenty-Four

Jiggling his leg, Ewan sat in Mr. Wilson's office. He'd let Daria go with her stepmother against his better judgment. The woman could not be trusted, of that he had no doubt. Her performance at the courthouse was contrived. It had to be. He might accept her sudden change of behavior if she'd said anything about becoming a believer in God, but the claim was decisively missing.

Daria would tell him to be less cynical about the woman, but he'd seen too many people like her, deceitful and manipulative, playing with others' emotions to get their way. She knew she was one step away from jail, so she'd changed her tune, acting like she'd been duped by someone else. No one bothered to explain who was supposed to have created the forged will and why they did it. Just like in Scotland, if a person had enough money, their problems could go away with the snap of a finger.

Is that what had happened to Da? Had one of the gentry bought their way out of trouble by implicating his father? A fragile theory but worth pursuing. He'd send a telegram to Mr. Nesmith as soon as Daria returned.

He glanced at the clock on the wall. The hands had barely moved since he'd last checked the time. He huffed out a deep breath and clenched his hands in his lap. He'd pace, but the movement wouldnae bring her back any sooner and would probably annoy the attorney who was hunched over his desk sifting through a stack of papers, periodically scribbling a note in the margin.

Outside, frenetic barking mingled with the wild clanging of a bell. He jumped up and raced to the window as the town's steam-powered fire engine clattered past, drawn by a trio of muscular horses. Two Dalmatians galloped beside the vehicle, baying their excitement. The New York Fire Department began using the sleek, spotted dogs a handful of years ago, and the idea caught on across the country. Someone discovered the breed quickly and strongly bonded with the horses, holding them in place during the chaos at the scene. The Dalmatians were also known to keep crowds of onlookers out of the way.

Ewan craned his neck, but the vehicle rounded the corner at the end of the block and disappeared from view. He opened the door and sniffed the air. The acrid smell of smoke floated on the breeze. His stomach clenched. A breeze could cause the fire to jump from house to house like the fire in Chicago two years ago. If that happened, Newport could be a pile of ash in a matter of hours.

"Mr. Wilson, I'm going to help put out the fire." Ewan grabbed one of two heavy wooden buckets painted with the attorney's name and address.

"I'm with you." The man stripped his jacket, tossed it on the desk, and snatched the second bucket off the hook, then slammed the door. "No time to waste."

They raced down the street, caught up in the horde of men also clutching pails and other receptacles. Pounding feet mingled with shouts as the mob turned the corner, then continued down the avenue. Black clouds rose above the roofline, and Ewan's pulse tripped. The fire appeared to be about four blocks away, the street on which Daria's childhood home stood. *Please, God, no!*

Churning his legs, he increased his pace and pushed his way to the front of the throng. His lungs and thighs burned, and his breath came in gasps, but he couldn't slow down, not until he knew Daria was safe. He'd stay to help even it wasn't her house on fire, but his heart knew he'd arrive and find the building in flames.

His feet chewed up the cobblestone street, and the gray veil of smoke infiltrated his nose and mouth. He coughed. His eyes began to sting, and tears streamed down his face. He whipped out his handkerchief and tied it across his face as did the men around him. He turned right at the next intersection, and his fears were confirmed.

Orange flames shot from the windows in the upper floor of Daria's family home. The once proud Greek Revival was now blackened and sagging. Two lines of men reached from the front door, across the street, down the grassy expanse to the rocky beach, passing full buckets from the ocean and returning the empty canisters to be refilled. An arc of water gushed through a leather hose from the pumper and doused the conflagration. Firefighters in heavy canvas coats dragged furniture onto the avenue.

"Daria!" His voice was ragged, as he searched the faces of the women clustered on one of the mansion's yards, watching the activity with wide eyes. His wife and her stepmother were conspicuously absent. His wife. Would he never get a chance to tell her she'd come to mean more to him than life? Would she be gone before she was truly his? He scrubbed at his face and heaved a sigh. He couldnae think like that, or he'd crumple to the ground writhing in the pain of a broken heart. Squaring his shoulders, he dashed toward the women. "Has anyone come out of the house? Have you seen Daria...Mrs. Mc—I mean Miss Burke or her stepmother. What of the girls?"

As one, they shrugged and shook their heads. He left them without a backward glance and sprinted to the front of the bucket brigade. "Where is the family? Has anyone gone inside to check for survivors?"

A towering, stocky man glowered at him. "The fire is too hot. It's too dangerous."

Ewan backed away, then looked up, searching the windows for signs that told him Daria or her family were trapped inside. On the second floor, a curtain moved, then his beloved's wan face appeared through the glass. She tugged at the window, but it didn't open. He nearly wept, instead waving his arms and heading back to the front door. "Upstairs! My wife is still in the house...upstairs," he panted. "We must get inside."

The man frowned and shook his head. "I told you it's too dangerous."

Ewan grabbed at the man's arm. "But she'll die if she doesn't get out."

"And you'll be killed if you try to make your way through the house." The fireman shook off Ewan's hand. "Now, get out of the way and let us do our jobs."

With a growl, Ewan whirled and went back to the street. He cupped his hands around his mouth and shouted, "I'm coming, Daria. Hold on!" He banged his hand on his chest, then pointed at her. "I'm coming."

He scrutinized the surrounding houses, the roar of the fire deafening. Fine mansions, every one of them, but were they too fancy to hold the one thing he needed? He darted back to the group of women. "Please tell me that one of your homes has a ladder tall enough to reach the second floor. I must get to my wife."

As one, the women gasped.

"Please." He held out his hands, beseeching them to focus on him. "I need your help."

A dumpy, gray-haired woman gestured to a federal-style white clapboard home. "I don't know if it will reach, but my maintenance man has one. He's here somewhere helping with the fire, but he keeps it in the basement."

Throat dry from terror and the smoke-filled air, Ewan croaked his thanks and barreled toward the magnificent structure. He circumvented the house and let himself in through the back gate, then hurried across the manicured lawn to an unobtrusive door on the corner. Would a two-story ladder fit inside the woman's house? He burst through the door and grinned. A huge wooden ladder lay along one wall. He should have known her cellar would be large enough to hold something of this length. He hefted it onto his shoulder and almost stumbled under the weight. Shifting his hold, he balanced it, then tramped out the door, grunting with exertion. Finally, when he could stand it no longer, he arrived back at the house. One of the men broke off from the brigade and rushed to his side. Together, they raised the ladder against the house. His companion steadied it, and Ewan clambered up the rungs.

As he reached the top, Daria managed to open the window and leaned out, sucking in loud breaths and hacking. Smoke billowed around her, and he shouted, "Are you injured? Can you climb over the sill?"

"I'm oka—" Overtaken by a paroxysm of coughing, she covered her mouth with both hands. An eternity later, she swallowed and reached for him.

He wrapped an arm around her waist as she slung first one leg, then the other over the sill in a swirl of skirts. She gripped the uprights, and he shielded her with his body. "I'll step down one rung at a time, and you follow. All right?"

Another nod, they crept to the ground, and Daria collapsed against him, her eyes rolling back into her head. Heart threatening to jump from his chest, he swept her into his arms. Did she still live?

Chapter Twenty-Five

Daria's eyelids fluttered open. The sun's glare pierced her eyes, and she moaned, closing them again, but not before she caught a glimpse of Ewan's worried face. The ground pressed against her legs, but the rest of her was cradled against his firm chest. A cozy, safe feeling enveloped her. She cracked open her eyes again, and this time she was able to keep them open. Ewan held one of his hands above her to shield the sun's rays. His expression was still one of apprehension, but a spark of hope glinted in his gaze. She sent him a smile, and the final vestiges of fear disappeared from his face.

He beamed, tears shimmering, then bent and brushed a kiss to her forehead. "Thank God you are okay, lass."

She sighed. Her throat and lungs burned with the words, and every muscle in her body ached. Her palms stung, but she would live. Her stepmother hadn't gotten away with her diabolical plan to kill her. Where was the woman? "Amaryllis?" She coughed, and Ewan held a glass of water to her lips. She sipped, the tepid liquid soothing her parched throat. The acrid smell of wet, burned wood clung to the air.

"In custody."

Realizing she still lay ensconced in Ewan's arms in public, Daria's face heated, and she struggled to sit up. "We shouldn't...uh...I should—"

"You are my wife, and I almost lost you. No one will judge us, and if they do, well, that's their problem." He nuzzled her neck.

She shivered, and her toes curled. Oh, how this man affected her. "You're right, but I am ready to sit somewhere else besides on the grass."

"Of course." He helped her to her feet, one strong arm wrapped around her waist. He guided her to a blue, floral Queen Anne chair that had been dragged from the house and braced her as she lowered herself onto the cushion.

A survey of the yard revealed a handful of pieces of furniture, looking quite out of place on the grassy lawn. Her gaze lifted to the house, the upper floor a charred shell with holes in the roof.

Her chin trembled. Father's beautiful home was destroyed. "After she locked me in the room, she said that if she couldn't have the house, then neither could I. Why would she do such a thing? Is she that bitter? I was going to give it to her. We don't need it." She turned to Ewan and searched his face. "How did you know she was responsible?"

"So many questions." He grinned and sat in the matching chair, leaning close enough to enfold her hands in his. His shirt was torn in several places, revealing glimpses of his bronzed torso. His hair stood on end, and black smudges of soot graced his cheeks and forehead. His teeth flashed white against his darkened face.

She dropped her gaze as warm tingles shot from her stomach to the tips of her fingers and toes. Only moments ago, she'd been encircled in his warm embrace relishing the feel of him against her. Would he think her improper if he could read her mind? She'd been nearly killed in a house fire, yet the only thing she cared about was the man sitting beside her. She must look a fright; however, his stare was not one of disgust or disappointment. His eyes sparkled, and his touch bordered on a caress.

With a calloused finger, he raised her chin. "Is there something on your mind, lass?" His eyebrows came together.

"So much, but I don't know where to start."

"I understand. A lot has happened. We'll take it one step at a time." He rubbed the back of her hand with his thumb. "I will tell you about Amaryllis, but it won't be easy to hear. As I said, she's been taken into custody, but it's most likely she'll end up in a hospital for the mentally ill."

"Hospital?" Daria gaped at him. "Why?"

"I overheard a couple of policemen. She was found sitting on the beach quite distraught. At first, it was thought she was upset about the fire, but she rambled nonstop, incoherently, and pulled at her hair and clothes. The only thing she said that did make sense was when she admitted to starting the fire. The police were called, and she was taken away, but she was accompanied by a doctor."

"How sad." She cocked her head. "You don't think it's another one of her acts to get sympathy, do you?"

"Not unless she's a better actress than we think, and, of course, that is possible." He heaved a sigh. "But the men I heard seemed to think there was nothing fake about her behavior."

"Where are the girls? They must be beside themselves with worry."

He shook his head. "Look at you. Barely out of a fire, and you're concerned about your stepsisters. Who, by the by, have treated you with nothing but contempt."

"True, but they don't deserve a mother who's gone insane. We should help them."

"We will, but that's for later." He stroked her jaw. "First, you must rest and focus on getting well. We're going to take you to the hospital to get examined, and then back to the hotel where you can lie down and recuperate."

Grabbing his fingers, she winced as her scraped palms protested, but continued to grasp his hand. "You should be checked as well. You've got several scrapes and cuts."

He winked. "Or you could nurse me back to health."

Her face heated, and a giggle escaped. "You're incorrigible."

"What?" He put on a mock expression of innocence. "It is not out of line for a husband to expect his wife to tend him in his hour of need."

She sent him a saucy grin. "Can a wife expect the same?"

A deep laugh rumbled in his chest, then he sobered and leaned forward, his gaze riveted on her face. A sheen formed in his eyes, and he swallowed. "I was terrified when I discovered you were in the house. I thought you wouldnae make it before I had a chance to tell you how I feel." He swallowed a second time. "I love you, Daria, with all my heart. You make me want to be a better man, a man you can be proud of. I've only known you a few weeks, yet I can't imagine my life without you." His smiled faltered. "I may be frightening you with my words, and you might not feel the same, but I cannae let another moment go by without telling you how much I love you—"

"Are you going to give me a chance to speak?" Daria smirked and pressed a finger on his lips. "I love you, too. When I thought I was going to die, I was devastated you wouldn't know. I scarcely believed it. It seemed too soon to have such strong feelings, but I—"

His lips came down on hers, and his arms engulfed her. His heart thudded against her chest as she snaked her arms around his neck. Her home was in ruins, but she had everything she needed in this man.

One year later

Epilogue

Golden sunlight cast long shadows across the churchyard as Daria cradled three-month-old Wilhelmina. Named for her mother-in-law, the baby had Ewan's nose and his grayish-blue eyes. Her wisps of blonde hair were the same color as Daria's. Willie, as they called her, chortled and waved her fists.

Daria kissed her daughter's head, then glanced across the grassy expanse. Children raced around the tables piled high with food while their parents chatted and laughed. Her gaze caught sight of Rayne and Flynn near the door to the church in conversation with her husband, and her heart swelled.

Her husband. In every sense of the word. And now he was a father. She loved watching him with Willie, his large hands cradling her like she was a fragile glass vase, his face glowing as if lit from within whenever he looked at her.

So much had happened since the fateful day of the fire. After a quick trip to the hospital, they'd returned to the hotel, and spent three days recuperating, languishing in each other's arms. Mr. Wilson had made arrangements for her accounts to be wired to the bank in Rocky Mountain Springs. Beyond repair, the house had been knocked down, and the land purchased by a man from Boston who knew her parents and had made his money in the Old China Trade like her father.

She and Ewan visited Amaryllis in the mental institute the day before they were to leave Newport, a difficult and disconcerting experience. At the sight of Daria, her stepmother had become highly agitated, her eyes wild and her words garbled. An orderly intervened and took the weeping woman away. Daria prayed daily that God would heal the woman's mind, but reports from the doctors thus far indicated no improvement.

When they'd arrived home, a wonderful surprise awaited them in the form of a telegram announcing that Ewan's father had been cleared of all charges. A series of events had shed light on the misdeeds of the man who had framed him, and within days, Tearlach had been released and his lands and title restored. She'd laughingly told Ewan she'd have married him sooner if she'd known he was going to be a duke.

Her father-in-law's adversary had been found guilty and jailed, and his properties and monies transferred to Ewan's father, who immediately booked passage to America for him and his wife. Tearlach and Wilhelmina had arrived just in time for Thanksgiving, and they agreed they had much to be thankful for. The couple was renting a house in town and had no plans to return to Scotland anytime soon.

Movement under the trees caught her attention, and she smiled at Pansy and Magnolia who strolled toward the church on the arms of their husbands obtained through the Westward Home and Hearts Agency that Ewan and the Wards had used.

The pastor from their church had ministered to them after Amaryllis was admitted to the hospital. He'd arranged for housing, and they received an allowance from the few funds their mother hadn't frittered away. At the Christmas service, they had each given their hearts to the Lord and written Daria to ask her forgiveness. She'd given it freely, and a flurry of letters passed between the three of them, drawing them closer than she'd ever imagined possible.

When she suggested they apply to Miss Crenshaw's agency, they jumped at the chance and specifically asked for husbands in Rocky Mountain Springs. Their double wedding occurred two months ago to the delight of the whole town.

Ewan hurried toward her, his face wreathed in smiles. Her pulse skittered. Even after more than a year of marriage, the man affected her like a schoolgirl, making her heart race. She sent him a wicked grin. "Are you enjoying the picnic, Your Grace?"

"I am." He snorted a laugh and bowed. "Being a duchess suits you. You look quite regal sitting there, but I thought we could take a turn around the yard." Desire darkened his eyes. "As lovely as this is, I'd like some time with my wife. Granted, we willnae exactly be alone, but at least we won't be overheard."

Her face heated. "And you planning to say scandalous things?"

"You can count on it. Now, pass Willie off to one of the ladies who will be thrilled to watch her for a bit. She shouldn't be privy to our conversation."

Daria's body trembled. Would she be able to walk without stumbling? "You're incorrigible."

"So you've said." He wiggled his eyebrows.

She rose, and they sauntered toward a cluster of women who argued good-naturedly over which one of them got to hold the baby first. Convinced Willie was in good hands, she looped her arm through the crook of Ewan's elbow, reveling in the feel of his muscled skin under her palm.

As they ambled away, he kissed her cheek. "Have I told you lately how much I love you?"

A giggle bubbled up. "Not in the last hour."

"Then I have been remiss." He pulled her close and squeezed her fingers. "And will take the rest of my life making up for it."

Her pulse thrummed. "A lifetime I look forward to."

THE END

What did you think of *Daria's Duke*?

Thank you so much for purchasing *Daria's Duke*. You could have selected any number of books to read, but you chose this book.

I hope it added encouragement and exhortation to your life. If so, it would be nice if you could share this book with your family and friends by posting to Facebook (www.facebook.com) and/or Twitter (www.twitter.com).

If you enjoyed this book and found some benefit in reading it, I'd appreciate it if you could take some time to post a review on Amazon, Goodreads, Kobo, Bookbub, GooglePlay, Apple Books, or other book review site of your choice. Your feedback and support will help me to improve my writing craft for future projects and make this book even better.
Thank you again for your purchase.

Blessings,
Linda Shenton Matchett

Grab your copy of the next installment of the
Westward Home & Hearts Mail Order Bride

Rachel's Refuge

Did you enjoy this installment of the *Westward Home & Hearts Mail-Order Brides* series? Read on for the first chapter of *Dinah's Dilemma*, another one of Linda's contributions to the series.

May 1870
Lincoln, Nebraska

Chapter One

Nathan Childs raced across the field toward his daughter as she toddled with determination toward the fire. How had he managed to let Florence get so far from his side? The three-year-old was fearless, and he knew better than to give her too much freedom. He'd already prevented her from crawling under the fence into the horse pen and trying to climb one of the massive sugar maples that sheltered the food tables at the town's Memorial Day celebration.

Perspiration trickled down his spine, and his shirt clung to his back as the midday sun beat down on his head and glared into his eyes. The morning had dawned unseasonably warm, and the temperatures continued to rise. Summers in Nebraska were known as scorchers, but May was early to be fighting heat and humidity.

"Florence," he shouted as he ran to gain the child's attention, but his voice was swallowed up in the myriad conversations, music, and laughter of Lincoln's citizens. Nebraska's capital had exploded in population over the last eighteen months, and Burlington and Missouri River Railroad's first train was due at the end of June. Sure to bring even more people. Not what he'd envisioned when he moved West after Georgianna's death.

Finally, close enough to grab her, he scooped Florence into his arms and pressed her close to his chest, her small body warm and soft. "What were you thinking, baby girl? Fire is bad. You need to be more careful and stay near me."

"No!" She arched her back and flailed her legs. "Fire is pretty, Daddy." Her face reddened, and she sobbed as if she'd lost her best friend. Tears dampened her cheeks, her blue eyes swimming.

His heart dropped. He hated when she cried. Her sobs made him feel as helpless as a newborn calf. He never knew what to do when she got like this. He hugged her closer and rubbed circles on her back in an effort to calm her.

"Sounds like someone's tired."

Nathan turned and nodded.

His best friend and the town sheriff, Alfred Denard, approached, a wide grin creasing his face below his black Stetson hat. "How about if you take a break and let Livvy watch her for a while. Looks like you both could use a change of scenery."

"Is it that obvious?"

Alfred chuckled as they headed for the cluster of women seated under the trees. "Sometimes I think you'd rather face the Mes Gang or Farrington Brothers than a crying little girl."

Nathan shrugged. "At least when I was chasing outlaws as a Pinkerton, I'd been trained and knew what to expect. Raising Florence is another whole ball of wax. Every day is different, so something I learned yesterday, doesn't necessarily work today." He blew out a deep breath as Florence quieted and tucked her thumb into her mouth. "I love her with my whole being, but maybe I should have let Georgianna's parents take her. I'm failing miserably."

"Do you think living with her grandparents is what's best for her?"

Nearing the blanket where Alfred's wife, Olivia, sat, Nathan paused and grimaced. "I don't know anymore. The thought of having to decide paralyzes me."

Livvy rose and held out her arms, her blonde hair swept into a tight bun at the base of her neck. She smiled, and her face glowed. "Are you going to let me spend time with your sweet little girl, Nathan? I've been aching to hold that child all day."

Florence chortled and reached for the buxom young woman. Nathan transferred his daughter into her waiting embrace, and his arms felt bereft. He shoved his hands into his pockets.

"Can I keep her through dinner, Nathan?" Livvy poked Florence's belly then rubbed noses with the giggling youngster. "We'll have lots of fun together, won't we?"

"You sure that's not too much time, Livvy?"

She shook her head. "Not enough, if you ask me." She jerked her head toward the corrals. "You boys head over to the pens and enjoy yourselves. The roping competitions should be starting soon."

Alfred ran his finger along her jaw then kissed her cheek, a starry-eyed look on his face. Married for three years, he still mooned over his wife, like a besotted schoolboy. Livvy had come from Atlanta as his friend's mail-order bride. Claiming love at first sight, they'd married immediately. "You holler if you need help, honey."

"I'll be fine." She winked at her husband. "Now, scoot."

Nathan pressed his lips together as his heart tugged. It had been too long since anyone looked at him like Livvy gazed at Alfred, but he had enough going on without saddling himself with a wife. He turned toward the festivities.

He couldn't ask for better friends than Alfred and Livvy. Two days after he'd arrived fifteen months ago, they'd shown up at his claim with food and friendship. Between the two of them, they'd arranged for some of the locals to transport his supplies from Omaha then pulled together a cadre of men to help build the house and barn. Livvy kept him fed when he didn't feel like eating in those early days of mourning after Georgianna's death. He'd figured moving to a new location would lessen the hollow feeling in his heart since she'd never lived in Nebraska, but his grief had followed him.

A city girl born and bred, she would have hated life on the plains, but he still missed her presence. Especially in the small things. Rustling up a stack of pancakes or sitting on the front porch watching the sun dip behind the trees, talking about everything and nothing.

The first year in Lincoln had been difficult, but rewarding. The crop had been decent, and he'd put aside some money for the future. Maybe to purchase the adjoining plot. Too soon to do so, but the idea was tempting. This year's wheat had done well and would be ready to harvest in another couple of months.

A stiff gust kicked up dust from the animal enclosures and swirled above the beasts. The acrid smell of manure clung to the breeze as it lifted his hat. Would he ever get used to the constant wind?

"All right, gents, time to see who's the best roper in the Lincoln." Barnard Johnson, a cattle rancher who owned the largest spread outside of town, stood in the center of one of the corrals, thumbs tucked in the waistband of his denim pants. A pair of ivory-handled pistols, Colts, if Nathan wasn't mistaken, hung from an ornate holster around his substantial belly. His boots gleamed.

Alfred jabbed Nathan with a sharp elbow. "You should take a turn. Show up the rest of the boys."

"No, thanks. I want to make friends not enemies."

"This is just a friendly competition."

"I'll pass, but you should take a turn. Confirm why you're the best sheriff in Nebraska."

"Because I can lasso the outlaws?" Alfred's chuckle rumbled in his chest. "Think I'll pass, too."

"Hey, Nathan. Aren't you going to show off those muscles of yours?"

Nathan cringed at the sound of Katrina Wainwright's strident voice that could send dogs and bats running for cover. She'd made her intentions clear at Christmas that he was the man for her despite his protestations to the contrary. Not one to be put off easily, she turned up at his side every chance she got. He squared his shoulders and pivoted on his heel.

Dipping his head in greeting, he forced a smile. "Good afternoon, Miss Wainwright. Are you enjoying today's event?"

Her giggle ended with a snort as she slapped his arm. "Katrina. How many times do I have to remind you to call me by my given name?"

"It wouldn't be proper, Miss Wainwright."

"We're not exactly in a Boston drawing room."

"True—"

"Hey, Katrina, watch this!" From inside the corral, one of Mr. Johnson's cowhands waved his hands over his head.

She turned, and Nathan took the opportunity to escape. Alfred followed close behind him. They strode to the six-foot tables piled with platters of food, grabbed a couple of plates, and chose several delicious-looking items. Nathan frowned. "That was a close one, but I feel bad for sneaking away."

"Don't. You've made it clear you're not interested. And after the incident with Florence when she took the child from the church nursery without your permission, she ought to know you'll never trust her." Alfred held an oatmeal cookie up to his nose and took a deep breath. "I do love my wife's baking." He took a bite and grinned. Shoving the rest of the treat into his mouth, he clapped Nathan on the back as he finished chewing. "I know how you can get rid of her."

Nathan narrowed his eyes. "I'm afraid to ask."

"Don't be. I have the perfect solution. You need a substitute girlfriend, and I know where you can get one."

"No. Before you say anything else, the answer is no. I'm not going to apply for a mail-order bride." Tears pricked the backs of his eyes. "You and Livvy are very happy, but I'm not in the market for a wife, and I don't think I'll ever be." He swallowed against the lump that had formed in his throat.

"I understand your grief. Don't forget I lost my first wife six years ago. But you can find love again. Unfortunately, the ratio of women to men out here isn't good, and your choices in Lincoln are limited." He wiggled his eyebrows. "Unless, you'd like to reconsider Miss Wainwright."

"Absolutely not." Nathan shuddered. "Despite her outward beauty, she's deceitful, and I could never love a woman like that. Florence and I are doing just fine with the two of us."

"Are you so sure about that? Your little girl needs a mother. You're not being fair to Florence. Please think about contacting Milly Crenshaw at the Westward Home and Hearts Matrimonial Agency." He squeezed Nathan's shoulder. "Now, as much as I enjoy time with you, I'm going to sit with my beautiful wife."

Nathan watched him leave, a jaunty air in his step as he threaded his way through the crowd to Livvy. She beamed as he approached then blushed after he bent and whispered something in her ear.

Was Alfred right? Could he find a woman he would love as he had Georgianna? He surveyed the townspeople, his gaze stopping to rest on Katrina. Full figured with a peaches-and-cream complexion, she had ebony-colored hair and deep-brown eyes. A gorgeous woman evidenced by the number of young men crowding around her like a flock of chicks.

But he couldn't get past her subterfuge. Plain and simple, she'd lied then claimed the whole thing was a misunderstanding. Should he try to find an honest woman who would love Florence as her own? Did this Milly Crenshaw have the answer? Surely, anyone she sent couldn't be any worse than Katrina.

Acknowledgments

Although writing a book is a solitary task, it is not a solitary journey. There have been many who have helped and encouraged me along the way.

My parents, Richard and Jean Shenton, who presented me with my first writing tablet and encouraged me to capture my imagination with words. Thanks, Mom and Dad!

Scribes212 – my ACFW online critique group: Valerie Goree, Marcia Lahti, and the late Loretta Boyett (passed on to Glory, but never forgotten). Without your input, my writing would not be nearly as effective.

Eva Marie Everson – my mentor/instructor with Christian Writers' Guild. You took a timid, untrained student and turned her into a writer. Many thanks!

SincNE, and the folks who coordinate the Crimebake Writing Conference. I have attended many writing conferences, but without a doubt, Crimebake is one of the best. The workshops, seminars, panels, critiques, and every tiny aspect are well-executed, professional, and educational.

Special thanks to Hank Phillippi Ryan, Halle Ephron, and Roberta Isleib for your encouragement and spot-on critiques of my work.

Thanks to my Book Brigade who provide information, encouragement, and support.

Paula Proofreader (https://paulaproofreader.wixsite.com/home): I'm so glad I found you! My work is cleaner because of your eagle eye. Any mistakes are completely mine.

A heartfelt thank you to my brothers, Jack Shenton and Douglas Shenton, and my sister, Susan Shenton Greger for being enthusiastic cheerleaders during my writing journey. Your support means more than you'll know.

My husband, Wes, deserves special kudos for understanding my need to write. Thank you for creating my writing room – it's perfect, and I'm thankful for it every day. Thank you for your willingness to accept a house that's a bit cluttered, laundry that's not always done, and meals on the go. I love you.

And finally, to God be the glory. I thank Him for giving me the gift of writing and the inspiration to tell stories that shine the light on His goodness and mercy.

Other Titles
Romance

Love's Harvest, Wartime Brides, Book 1

Love's Rescue, Wartime Brides, Book 2

Love's Belief, Wartime Brides, Book 3

Love's Allegiance, Wartime Brides, Book 4

Love Found in Sherwood Forest

A Love Not Forgotten

On the Rails

A Doctor in the House

Spies & Sweethearts, Sisters in Service, Book 1

The Mechanic & the MD, Sisters in Service, Book 2

The Widow & the War Correspondent, Sisters in Service, Book 3

Love at First Flight

Multi-author Series

A Bride for Seamus (Proxy Brides, 48)

A Bride for Seamus (Proxy Brides, 62)

Dinah's Dilemma (Westward Home and Hearts Mail-Order Brides, 10)

Rayne's Redemption (Westward Home and Hearts Mail-Order Brides, 15)

Legacy of Love (Keepers of the Light, 10)

Vanessa's Replacement Valentine, (Brides of Pelican Rapids, 13)

Gold Rush Bride Hannah (Gold Rush Brides, 1)

Gold Rush Bride Caroline (Gold Rush Brides, 2)

Mystery
Under Fire, Ruth Brown Mystery Series, Book 1

Under Ground, Ruth Brown Mystery Series, Book 2

Under Cover, Ruth Brown Mystery Series, Book 3

Murder of Convenience, Women of Courage, Book 1

Murder at Madison Square Garden, Women of Courage, Book 2

Non-Fiction
WWII Word Find, Volume 1

Biography

Linda Shenton Matchett writes about ordinary people who did extraordinary things in days gone by. She is a volunteer docent and archivist at the Wright Museum of WWII. Born in Baltimore, Maryland, a stone's throw from Fort McHenry, she has lived in historical places most of her life. Now located in central New Hampshire, Linda's favorite activities include exploring historical sites and immersing herself in the imaginary worlds created by other authors.

Website/blog: http://www.LindaShentonMatchett.com
Newsletter signup (receive a free short story):
https://mailchi.mp/74bb7b34c9c2/lindashentonmatchettnewsletter
Facebook: http://www.facebook.com/LindaShentonMatchettAuthor
Pinterest: http://www.pinterest.com/lindasmatchett
Amazon: https://www.amazon.com/Linda-Shenton-Matchett/e/B01DNB54S0
Goodreads: http://www.goodreads.com/author_linda_matchett
Bookbub: http://www.bookbub.com/authors/linda-shenton-matchett